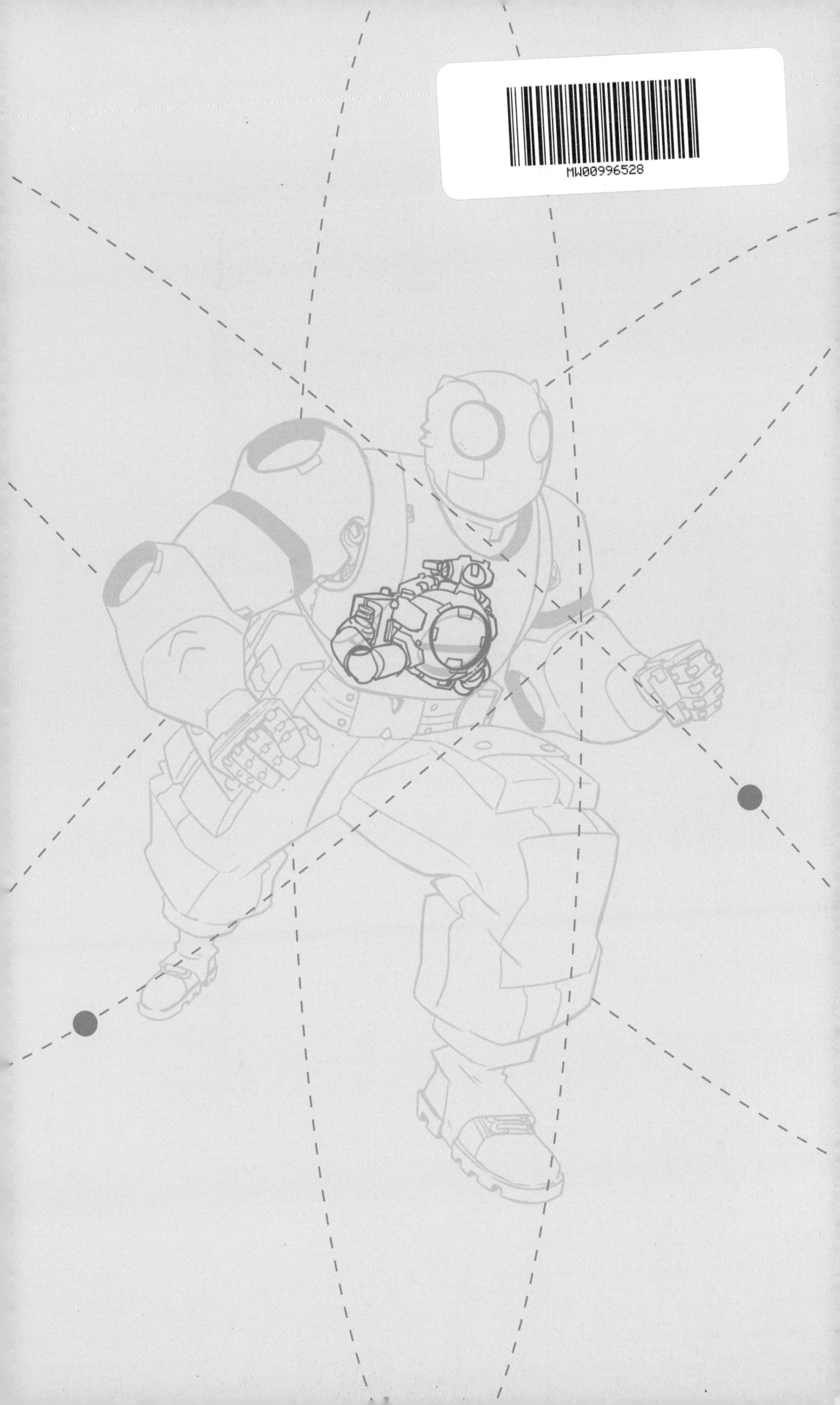

IDW

Facebook: **facebook.com/idwpublishing**
Twitter: **@idwpublishing**
YouTube: **youtube.com/idwpublishing**
Tumblr: **tumblr.idwpublishing.com**
Instagram: **instagram.com/idwpublishing**

COVER ART BY
SCOTT WEGENER
AND ANTHONY CLARK

COLLECTION EDITS BY
JUSTIN EISINGER
AND ALONZO SIMON

COLLECTION DESIGN BY
JEFF POWELL

PUBLISHER
TED ADAMS

ISBN: 978-1-63140-863-2 20 19 18 17 1 2 3 4



Originally published as ATOMIC ROBO: THE TEMPLE OF OD issues #1–5.



TESLADYNE LLC

AND

# THE TEMPLE OF OD

WORDS
**BRIAN CLEVINGER**

ART
**SCOTT WEGENER**

CREATORS

COLORS
**ANTHONY CLARK**

LETTERS
**JEFF POWELL**

EDITS
**LEE BLACK**

Here's the thing about *Atomic Robo*: it's impossible to describe in a meaningful way because it is simply too epic of a work to find a meaningful way to dissect it. Though, one would assume that I could do this because I was asked too—so, I can try, right?

Here goes.

The work from Clevinger, Wegener, and Clark on *Atomic Robo* succeeds because it manages to be a taut, modern action comedy, while simultaneously pushing the most accurate, jargon-laden science fiction this side of anything being published in comics right now, and all of that somehow manages to fit into the time period that the story is being told from. Clevinger's ability to match the scuttlebutt (See what I did there? That's 1940s argot) of the time period he's operating in is second to none. This is then amplified by Wegener's stunning ability to recreate the visuals of that particular time and setting. In the case of this volume, we start in Manchukuo, in and of itself a puppet-state of both China and Mongolia until the start of the second World War (WHO IS QUALIFIED TO WRITE AN INTRODUCTION TO THIS?).

Oh, and Anthony Clark's color-work is beautiful, subtle, and reserved—which is the perfect way to ground a comic about a robot jaunting through a discombobulated alternate-history of Tesla, Edison, and any number of other geniuses of their time period with a believable sense of place.

Yeah, you could say I'm a fan.

What continues to stagger me about the books is each volume sets out to do something completely different. In this volume, you get a rousing desert epic with tanks and tank-punching, a respectful, deep dissection of an Asian-continental subculture that I didn't even know existed until I read this volume (and did ample research just to write this gosh-danged foreword,) some of the best dialog-work, probably that Brian has ever done, and somehow, at the end of it, you're still just a five-year-old kiddo delighting in the madness of the robot man kick-fighting his way across Asia.

Like, I need a breather just talking about this. How did human people even make this?

Short answer: I couldn't.

And that's why I adore it.

Mikey Neumann
(Borderlands *writer and creator of* Movies with Mike)

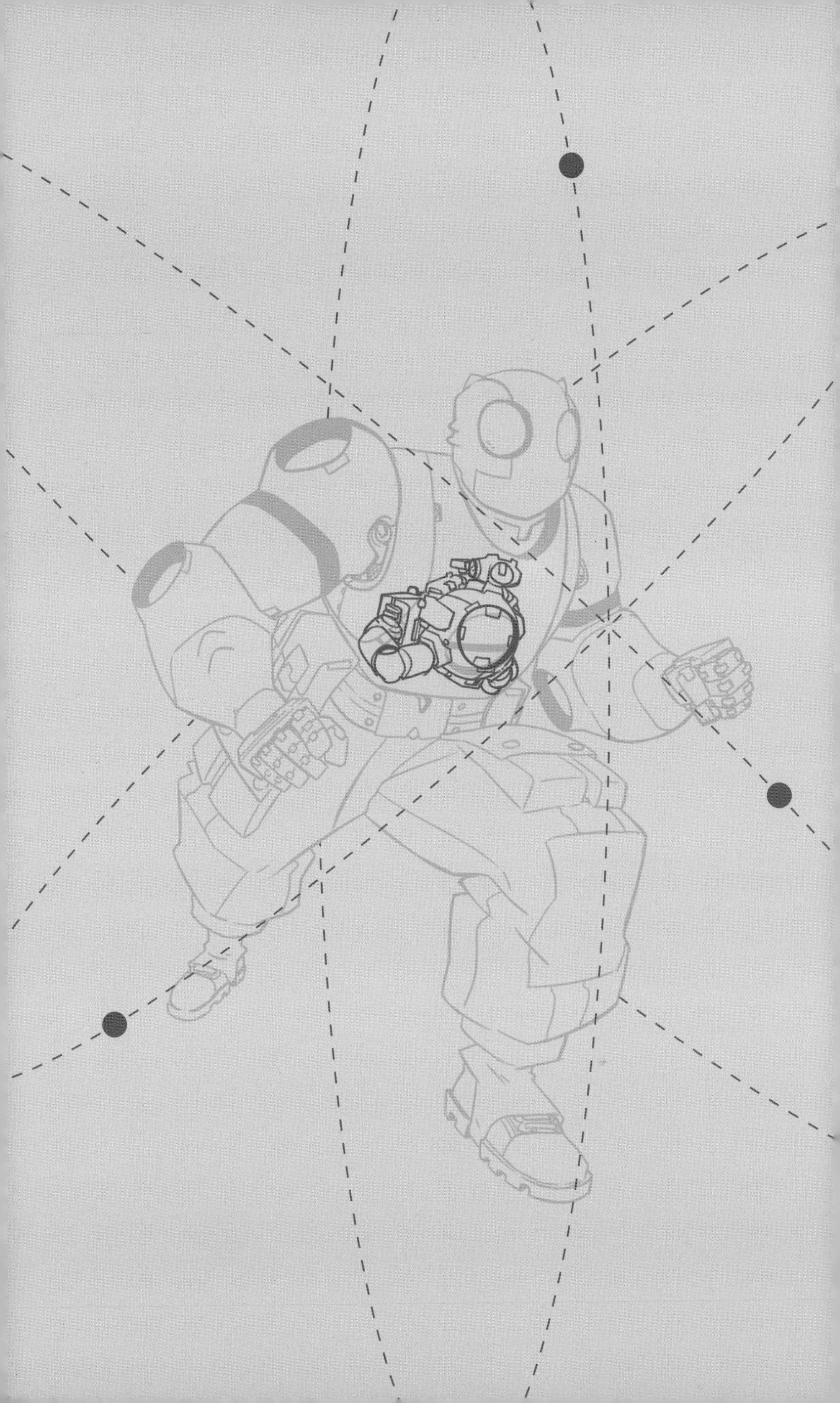

# 1

# ONCE UPON A TIME IN MANCHURIA

ART BY SCOTT WEGENER
COLORS BY ANTHONY CLARK

MANCHUKUO, 1938
I DON'T WANT TO ALARM YOU, BUT I *THINK* THEY'RE GETTING CLOSER.

BOOOM
*WHAT TIPPED YOU OFF?*

<THEY CANNOT BE ALLOWED TO ESCAPE!>
VRRMMMM

TRY MISSING A **FEW** BUMPS SO I CAN TAKE A SHOT!
*NOT A LOT OF **ROAD** OUT HERE.*
**IMPROVISE!**

*OKAY, BUT YOU WON'T LIKE IT.*
WAIT. WHY NOT?

YOU WERE RIGHT!
DON'T WORRY, THIS ISN'T THE BAD PART!

THIS BETTER BE IT!
DEPENDS ON THE LANDING.
BANG
BANG

ZPWING
PWANG
TWONK

KRAK
BOOOM
KRONCH

D'OOF!
FWUMP

BAD NEWS. DROPPED THE GUNS.
WHAT'S THE GOOD NEWS?
NO MORE TANKS.

PFOOOM
THE HECK IS *THAT?*
LET'S NOT WAIT AROUND TO FIND OUT.

SKRSHHHH

KTHOOOM

KUNMING, TWO MONTHS EARLIER

GENERAL CHENNAULT, SIR? YOU WANTED TO SEE ME.

AT EASE. GOT A MISSION FOR YOU.

UH. I DID MY MISSION, SIR.
Y'DID. THIS ONE'S NEXT.

THE JAPANESE HAVE A VRIL WEAPON PROGRAM?
SOMETHING LIKE IT. EVER HEAR OF DOCTOR LU HUANG?
DON'T THINK SO.

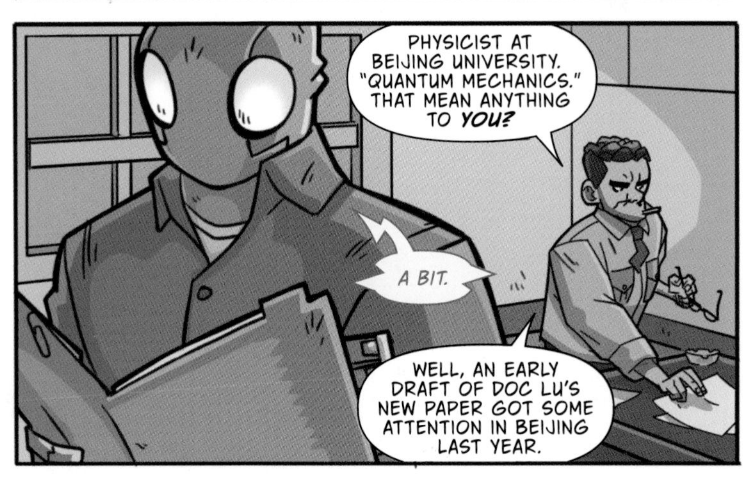
PHYSICIST AT BEIJING UNIVERSITY. "QUANTUM MECHANICS." THAT MEAN ANYTHING TO YOU?
A BIT.
WELL, AN EARLY DRAFT OF DOC LU'S NEW PAPER GOT SOME ATTENTION IN BEIJING LAST YEAR.

"HYPERGEOMETRIC LOOP LENSING EFFECTS ON ZERO-POINT ENERGY CONDENSATES."

THAT MEAN SOMETHING TO YOU TOO?
COULD MEAN A LOT OF THINGS. I'D HAVE TO SEE THE MATH.
WE'RE LUCKY TO HAVE THE TITLE.

OUR EGGHEADS WERE SAYING THAT PAPER WOULDA MADE LU MORE FAMOUS THAN EINSTEIN IF HE'D PUBLISHED IT.
YEAH? WHY DIDN'T HE?
THE JAPANESE INVADED. BEIJING WAS THEIR FIRST TARGET. DOCTOR LU AND ALL HIS WORK DISAPPEARED.

OKAY. DON'T TELL ME. NOW THERE ARE REPORTS OF THE JAPANESE DEVELOPING ZERO-POINT TECHNOLOGY.
REPORTS YOU WILL INVESTIGATE.

WELL, SIR. LIKE I SAID. I AGREED TO ONE MISSION. AND IT'S DONE.
DONE? NOTHING'S DONE, ROBO.

MAYBE THIS IS NEWS TO YOU, BUT TOJO'S NOT GONNA STOP WITH CHINA ANY MORE THAN ADOLF'S GONNA STOP WITH EUROPE.

THE JAPANESE ARE TURNING DOCTOR LU'S THEORIES INTO SOME KIND OF TELEFORCE GUN.
YES. LIKE TESLA'S. THAT GET YOUR ATTENTION?

YOU'LL MEET OUR CONTACT WITH THE RESISTANCE IN SHANGHAI. THEY'LL GET YOU TO BEIJING TO FIND DOCTOR LU.
YOU WILL DESTROY THE JAPANESE TELEFORCE PROJECT BY ANY MEANS NECESSARY.
AND WHEN THAT'S DONE, WE'LL DO WHAT COMES NEXT.

I DON'T EXACTLY BLEND IN.

YOU'RE A GLOBETROTTING MILLIONAIRE ADVENTURER.
SHANGHAI'S THE ONE PLACE YOU WON'T STAND OUT.

EVEN SO. THE JAPANESE WILL WATCH ME LIKE A HAWK.
HELL, WE'RE COUNTING ON IT. THE MORE THEY WATCH YOU, THE EASIER IT'LL BE FOR THE RESISTANCE TO ROOT OUT SYMPATHIZERS.

SHANGHAI, ONE MONTH LATER

SHOESHINE, MISTER?
YEAH, OKAY.

CREAK

YOU BROKE IT YOU BOUGHT IT, PAL.
YOUR ENGLISH IS PRETTY GOOD.

NOT BAD YOURSELF.
SHUFF
SHUFF
FWIP

SO. UH.
SEEN THE NEW FRED ASTAIRE PICTURE?
SNAP

YOU DON'T HAVE TO DO THE CODE PHRASE.
NO?

THERE AREN'T TOO MANY PEOPLE YOU CAN BE.
YEAH, I GUESS NOT.
FWUP
SHUFF

THINK I'M BEING WATCHED.

YEAH, DEFINITELY. YOU'RE FUNNY LOOKING.
OKAY, DONE. GET UP. QUICK BEFORE YOU BREAK THE CHAIR.

YOU GOT A REAL WAY WITH CUSTOMERS, KID.

THEY MUST NOT PAY ROBOTS TOO MUCH, HUH?
WHERE AM I HEADED?
ANYTHING GOES. THREE BLOCKS SOUTH. CAN'T MISS IT.
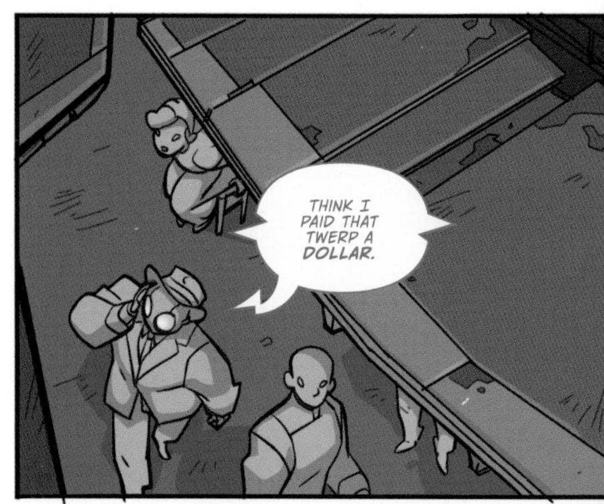
THINK I PAID THAT TWERP A DOLLAR.

THREE BLOCKS TO THE SOUTH...
舞蹈
ANYTHING GOES
CLUB
YEAH. THERE'S NO MISSING THAT.

CIGARETTE?
NO THANKS.
YOU SURE? TAKE A GOOD LOOK.

TRYING TO CUT DOWN.

OH.

JUST ACT NATURAL.

AND LOOK UP WITHOUT LOOKING UP.

D'AH!

CRASH

<HE PUSHED ME!>

UH. HEY. WAIT A MINUTE.

Y'GOT THE WRONG IDEA!

I CAN *EXPLAIN!*

JUST SEND ME THE CLEANING BILL. WE'LL CALL IT EVEN.
THIS WAY.

*HE* BUMPED INTO *ME*, Y'KNOW.
THIS WAY.

MR. CHEN.

THE TRIADS ARE KNOWN TO HAVE TIES TO THE RESISTANCE. WE HAD TO MAKE SURE THE JAPANESE THINK YOU'RE NO FRIEND OF OURS.

THEN YOU'RE MY CONTACT?
I'M CHEN ZHEN. AGAINST THE JAPANESE, I'M EVERYONE'S CONTACT.
AWFULLY PUBLIC VENUE, ISN'T IT?

IT IS. THE IMPERIAL ARMY THINKS THEY GET VALUABLE INFORMATION BY KEEPING AN EYE ON US, SO THEY NEVER RAID THE CLUB.
MEANWHILE WE KEEP OUR REAL OPERATIONS OUT OF THEIR SIGHT.

OF COURSE, TO MAINTAIN THE CHARADE, WE HAVE TO LET THEM FIND SOMETHING EVERY SO OFTEN.
LIKE A FOREIGN AGENT.

AND HERE I THOUGHT WE WERE ON THE SAME SIDE.

ARE WE?
YOU TELL ME. I'M HERE TO DESTROY THE JAPANESE TELEFORCE WEAPON.
YES, AS A PRETEXT FOR FINDING DOCTOR LU SO HE CAN BUILD ONE FOR YOUR GOVERNMENT.

THAT HADN'T OCCURRED TO YOU?
ROBO, WE'RE FIGHTING A WAR, BUT OUR LEADERS ARE FIGHTING THE NEXT ONE. YOU CAN'T AFFORD TO BE NAIVE.

YEAH, WELL, I'M NEW TO THIS STUFF. ALL I KNOW IS THAT ZERO-POINT ENERGY IS THEORETICALLY LIMITLESS.
IF DOCTOR LU'S THEORIES WORK OUT, THEN IT'S NOT A WEAPON, IT'S A DOOMSDAY DEVICE. IT COULD CRACK THE PLANET IN HALF.

I NEED YOUR SPY NETWORK TO HELP ME SHUT IT DOWN AND RESCUE LU SO THAT DOESN'T HAPPEN.
I DON'T CARE WHAT WE DO WITH HIM FROM THERE. YOU CAN MAKE HIM DISAPPEAR. I'LL TELL MY SUPERIORS HE DIED.
WHATEVER IT TAKES TO KEEP HIS IDEAS FROM SPREADING.

WHAT'S TO STOP ME FROM TURNING HIM IN TO MY GOVERNMENT?
I'M JUST A NAIVE MORON, BUT I DON'T TRUST ANY NATION WITH THAT KIND OF POWER.
DO YOU?

NO. I DON'T. BUT YOU ARE NAIVE. YOU SHOULDN'T TRUST ME YET.
WELL, START EARNING MY TRUST THEN.
OKAY. LET'S GO TO THE KITCHEN.

SHANGHAI IS THE HEART OF THE RESISTANCE. I'M ITS FACE.

YOU SHOULD MEET ITS NERVE CENTER.

IMPRESSIVE SET UP.
WE HAVE STATIONS LIKE THIS IN EVERY OCCUPIED CITY. FROM HERE WE COORDINATE THE RESISTANCE AND GATHER INTEL ALL ACROSS CHINA.
THAT'S HOW WE LEARNED ABOUT THIS RESEARCH PROJECT IN MANCHUKUO FOR "SPECIAL GUN NUMBER TWO."

ROBO, MEET--
HELEN?!

ROBO?!

YOU KNOW EACH OTHER?

YEAH, WE USED TO--
KNOW EACH OTHER. FROM YEARS BACK.
UH. OKAY.

WHAT ARE YOU DOING HERE?
WHAT ARE YOU DOING HERE?

TIBET. ZEN MARKS-MANSHIP. JAPANESE INVASION. STUCK IN SHANGHAI.

DIDN'T TAKE LONG TO COME ACROSS THE RESISTANCE. AND ZHEN.
AND HERE WE ARE.
OH. I SEE.

CHENAULT SENT ROBO TO HELP US GET DOCTOR LU AND HIS ZERO-POINT ENERGY WEAPON. GIVE HIM THE BRIEF.
THE GOOD NEWS IS, WE THINK WE KNOW WHERE HE IS. THEY'VE SENT A DOZEN QUANTUM MEN TO THIS ONE REMOTE RESEARCH STATION.
AND THEY'VE BEEN REQUISITIONING ALL KINDS OF BIZARRE STUFF LIKE SELENIUM CORED GIRDERS AND MAGNESIUM-TUNGSTEN ALLOYS.

REMEMBER EDISON'S ODIC MACHINE?
OF COURSE. IT HARNESSED HIDDEN ENERGIES. UNTIL IT EXPLODED.
MR. TESLA AND I EXAMINED THE REMAINS. IT HAD A SELENIUM CORE SUSPENDED IN A MAGNESIUM-TUNGSTEN CAGE.

THAT'S TOO MUCH OF A COINCIDENCE TO BE A CO-INCIDENCE.

WHAT'S AN ODIC MACHINE?
EDISON THOUGHT IT WOULD COLLECT THIS MYSTERIOUS ENERGY HE DISCOVERED AND MAKE HIM IMMORTAL.
BUT, LIKE MR. TESLA SAYS, SCIENCE IS NOT AN EXACT SCIENCE.

MAYBE EDISON DISCOVERED DOCTOR LU'S ZERO-POINT ENERGY WITHOUT KNOWING IT.
THAT WOULD EXPLAIN THE ENORMOUS EXPLOSION.

YEAH. IF ZERO-POINT ENERGY IS EVEN A FRACTION AS ENERGETIC AS ODIC FORCE--
<MR. CHEN! IT'S A RAID!>

GET ROBO OUT OF HERE.
I'M NOT LEAVING YOU!

HELEN. I CAN'T TRUST ANYONE *ELSE.*
GET HIM TO DOCTOR LU.

WHAT ABOUT *YOU?*
I WON'T BE FAR BEHIND.

LIAR.

MMPH!

I SHOULD SEE YOU FOR THE LAST TIME MORE OFTEN.
*NOT* FUNNY.

NO, THAT WAS A PRETTY GOOD LINE.
BOP
C'MON.

IT'S A MAZE DOWN HERE. STAY CLOSE.

MANCHUKUO
<PICK HER UP.>

WHUD

KCHK

YEAH, YOU MIGHT GET *ME.* BUT ROBO'S *BULLETPROOF.*

UH.
ABOUT THAT.

OH.
OH, I SEE.

TNK

<SEARCH HER FOR WEAPONS.>
<YES, LIEUTENANT.>

<AND KEEP AT LEAST **THREE** GUNS POINTED AT HER AT ALL TIMES.>

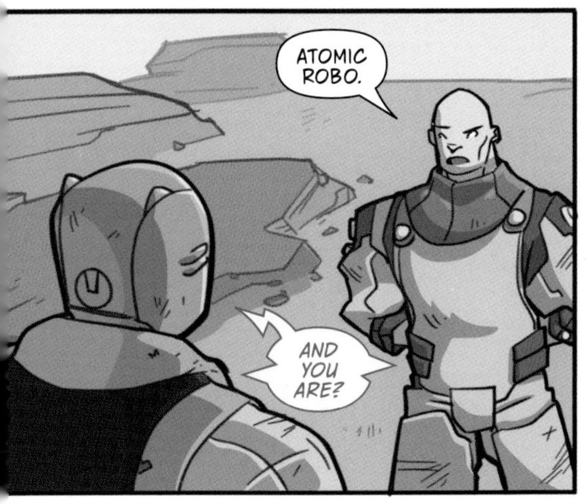
ATOMIC ROBO.
*AND YOU ARE?*

LIEUTENANT MATSUDA ICHIRO.
*NOT MANY FOLKS CAN DO WHAT YOU DID BACK THERE.*
NOT YET, NO.

WHO THOUGHT IT WAS A GOOD IDEA TO SEND THE MOST FAMOUS FACE IN THE HISTORY OF THE WORLD ON A **SPY** MISSION?

*AH. WELL, I'M NOT A SPY. I'M AN **ADVENTURER.** EVERYONE KNOWS THAT.*
THEN IT IS ONLY **COINCIDENCE** THAT YOU ARE "ADVENTURING" WITH ONE OF CHEN ZHEN'S INNER CIRCLE?

*MS. McALLISTER? SHE'S A MILLIONAIRE SOCIALITE. **AND** AN ADVENTURER IN HER OWN RIGHT. I CAN'T ACCOUNT FOR EVERYONE SHE'S MET.*

WE TRACKED YOU **BOTH** FROM THE RESISTANCE IN **SHANGHAI** TO **BEIJING** TO OUR REMOTE AND **VERY** SECRET MANCHUKUO RESEARCH FACILITY.
**ALL** COINCIDENCE?

MUST BE.
AND YOU PROBABLY SHOULDN'T **ADMIT** THE FACILITY IS **REAL** IF IT'S A **SECRET**.

IS HE **ALWAYS** THIS INANE?

HEY! I JUST REALIZED WE HAVE THE **SAME** BARBER!

I **WAS** FEELING BAD ABOUT DISSECTING YOU. THANK YOU FOR FIXING THAT.

<RADIO HEADQUARTERS. TELL THEM WE HAVE THE SPIES.>

# THE GOOD, THE BAD, AND THE ROBOT

2

ART BY SCOTT WEGENER
COLORS BY ANTHONY CLARK

SIHANG WAREHOUSE, SHANGHAI
OCTOBER 28, 1937
<THEY SAID THE INVADERS COULDN'T BE STOPPED.>
<UNTIL WE STOPPED THEM.>
LT. COL. XIE JINYUAN

<DONE YET?>
CHEN ZHEN

<ALMOST.>
HELEN "THE NIGHTINGALE" McALLISTER
ACROSS FROM SIHANG WAREHOUSE

<HOW ALMOST ARE WE TALKING?>
<I DON'T NEED TO REMIND YOU THERE'S BOUND TO BE MORE ON THE WAY.>

<I'D BE GOING FASTER IF YOU WEREN'T MAKING SUCH A RACKET.>
<YOU'VE GOT MORE FRIENDS, BY THE WAY.>

<I'LL TRY TO KEEP THE NOISE DOWN.>

<DO YOU KNOW WHAT THEY'RE CALLING US? THE EIGHT HUNDRED **HEROES.**>

HHHUK!
FWACKT

<**WE** ARE SHANGHAI'S FINAL HOPE.>

<CAREFUL, CHEN!>

<I GOT IT.>
**AUGH!**
<**THREE'S** TOO MANY!>

<AND SHANGHAI IS **CHINA'S** FINAL HOPE.>

<WON'T BE **THREE** OF THEM FOR LONG.>

CH-CHAK
?

OH.

<HOW CAN WE REPEL THE INVADERS WHEN WE CAN'T EVEN KEEP THE LIGHTS ON?>

<THE BREAKER'S ARE FIXED.>
<AND I **TOLD** YOU THREE WAS TOO MANY.>

<GOOD THING I BROUGHT HELP.>

<EVERY HOUR WE RESIST THE INVADERS IS AN HOUR CLOSER TO **VICTORY.**>

MANCHUKUO, 1938
SO.
YOU AND CHEN.
ME AND CHEN. DO YOU LIKE HIM?

ME? DO YOU LIKE HIM?
HE SEEMS NICE.
YEAH. A LOT.
HE IS.

THINK THERE'S A FUTURE THERE?
COULD BE. SHANGHAI'S FULL OF COUPLES LIKE US.

YOU'LL STAY THERE?
MAYBE. I DON'T KNOW.
IS THIS WEIRD? FOR US, I MEAN. TALKING ABOUT HIM.

MAYBE. BUT WE WERE ALWAYS A LITTLE WEIRD.
A LITTLE VERY WEIRD.

YEAH. WE WERE GREAT, BUT...WEIRD.
I'M GLAD YOU FOUND SOMEONE YOU CAN HAVE A FUTURE WITH.
THAT'S ASSUMING I'VE GOT A FUTURE AT ALL.

WHAT, THIS? DON'T WORRY.
THEY CAN'T KILL YOU. IF THEY DO, THERE'S NOTHING HOLDING ME BACK.

THAT'S NOT EXACTLY A RELIEF.
I SUPPOSE NOT.

BUT THIS IS THE PART OF THE PLAN WHERE WE WAIT FOR AN OPPORTUNITY TO MAKE OUR MOVE.
PROBABLY A BIT OPTIMISTIC TO CALL WHAT'S HAPPENING RIGHT NOW A PLAN.
LIKE HOW DID MATSUDA KNOCK YOU AROUND LIKE THAT?

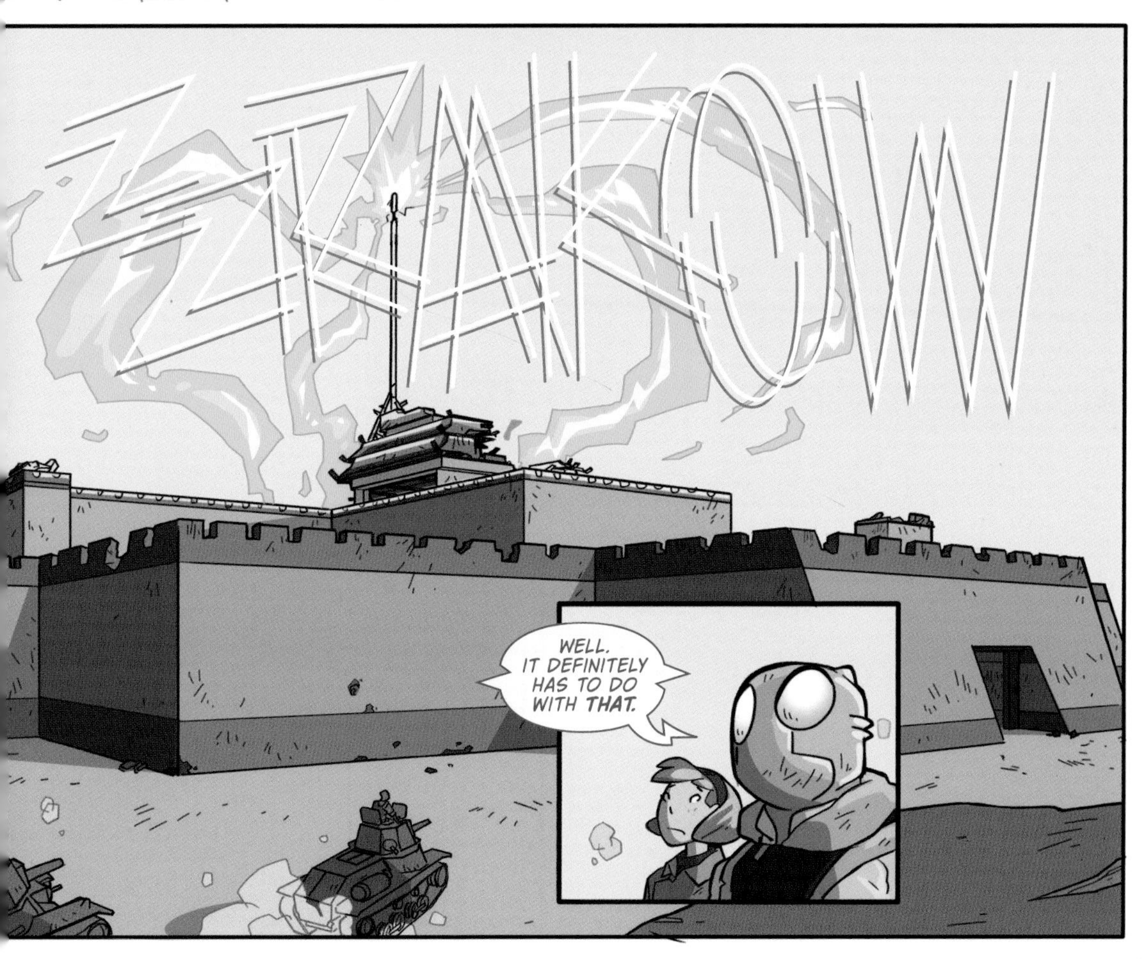
WELL. IT DEFINITELY HAS TO DO WITH THAT.

<NEVER SEEN LIGHTNING LIKE THAT.>
<IS IT LIGHTNING?>

<SO, WHAT'S THE PLAY HERE? WE DOIN' THIS?>
<WE HAVE TO.>
<THE HELL WE DO. WE'RE THE GHOST BANDITS, NOT THE CHIVALRY GANG.>

<WE FOLLOWED THE WOMAN AND HER ROBOT. NOW ALL WE HAVE TO DO IS TELL CHEN'S PEOPLE WE FOUND THE BASE THEY'RE LOOKING FOR.>
<IF CHEN WANTS IT SO BAD, HE CAN GET HIS OWN HANDS DIRTY FOR A CHANGE.>

<SEE, THAT'S WHY YOU AREN'T THE LEADER OF THIS OUTFIT. THIS ONE RAID CAN SCORE US THREE FORTUNES.>

<THINK IT THROUGH. THAT IS A TOP SECRET MILITARY RESEARCH STATION. WHATEVER THEY'RE DOING IN THERE IS WORTH MILLIONS.>
<IF WE CAN TAKE IT, CHEN WILL HAVE TO PAY US WHATEVER WE ASK TO GET AT IT. BUT WE'LL ALSO RANSOM IT BACK TO THE JAPANESE.>
<AND THEY'LL KILL EACH OTHER FIGHTING OVER IT! BUT WHAT'S THE THIRD FORTUNE?>

<WHEN THE DUST SETTLES WE KILL THE WINNER AND SELL OUT TO WHOEVER COMES NEXT. RUSSIANS PROBABLY.>

<ONE RAID. THREE FORTUNES.>
<WE HAVE TO DO THIS!>

WHERE DO YOU THINK THEY'RE KEEPING DOCTOR LU?

WHAT WE'RE ***SEEING*** IS A MILITARY BASE. BUT WE KNOW IT'S A RESEARCH STATION. THAT PART'S PROBABLY UNDER-GROUND.
THAT'S WHERE HE'LL BE.

SILENCE.
<YOU THERE. THE WOMAN IS WITH THE RESISTANCE. PREPARE AN INTERROGATION ROOM.>
<AS FOR ATOMIC ROBO...>

WHAT ***ARE*** WE TO DO WITH YOU?
SHOULD'VE THOUGHT OF ***THAT*** BEFORE YOU ***CAPTURED*** ME.

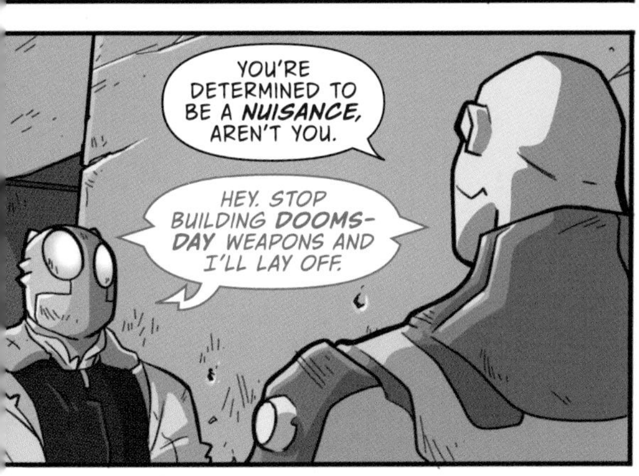
YOU'RE DETERMINED TO BE A ***NUISANCE,*** AREN'T YOU.
HEY. STOP BUILDING ***DOOMS-DAY*** WEAPONS AND I'LL LAY OFF.

IS ***THAT*** WHAT YOU THINK WE'RE DOING HERE?

KRAKOOOOM

FOR SOME ***CRAZY*** REASON, YES.

THAT? HARMLESS.
A MERE BY-PRODUCT OF OUR WORK.

WE ARE EXPLORING THE MEREST SCRAP OF WHAT CAN BE ACCOMPLISHED WITH DOCTOR LU'S THEORIES.
IN TIME, WE WILL UNLOCK ULTIMATE POWER OVER THE FABRIC OF THE UNIVERSE.

Y'KNOW. I BLEW UP THE LAST TWO GUYS WHO TALKED TO ME LIKE THAT.
MATSUDA HERE MIGHT BE YOUR CHANCE TO CATCH UP.
TWO? GOSH, I'M FALLING BEHIND.

AND HOW DO YOU PROPOSE TO DO THAT FROM CAPTIVITY?

BOOM

BKOOM
BANG
<DIRECT HIT!>

CREEEAAAK

FWAK
CHANK

<TAKE THEM TO THE CELLS. I WILL DEAL WITH THESE-->

FWAM

UH. ROBO?

SKROOOM

BAFOOOM

CHAKKA CHAKKA
VROOOM
CHATTA CHATTA
BANG
BKOW

<SECURE THE LABS!>

<PUSH THEM BACK!>
CKRUNCH

HEY. WE'RE ALIVE.
YES, BUT ONE OF US NEEDS TO BREATHE.
I MIGHT HAVE SOME GOOD NEWS ABOUT THAT.
DO TELL.

MY HAND'S FREE.

WELL. THAT BOUGHT US A FEW MINUTES.

GOTTA SAY, THIS DOESN'T LOOK LIKE A LAB.
YEAH, MUST BE SOME KINDA STORAGE BASEMENT. IT COULD TAKE US HOURS TO FIND DOCTOR LU.

OR, UH, A FEW SECONDS.

KRAKABOOOM

ARGH!
<GOT 'EM!>
DAKKA DAKKA
BLAM BLAM

CHATTA
<ONE RAID!>
<THREE FORTUNES!>
BKAM

<THEIR VEHICLES! AIM FOR THEIR VEHICLES!>
CHAKKA

<HUNGER HAS MADE BOLD WOLVES OUT OF OUR WASTELAND DOGS.>
<SLAUGHTER THEM.>

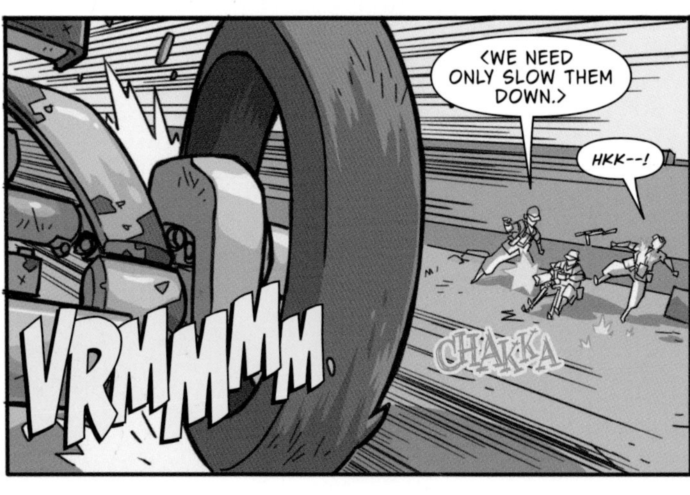
<WE NEED ONLY SLOW THEM DOWN.>
HKK--!
VRMMMM
CHAKKA

CHAKKA

THWAK

THUD

FWAM
ARGH!
CRONCH
MY BONES!

WE'RE THE GOOD GUYS.
HONEST. THEY *MADE* US DO THAT.

IS THIS A RESCUE?
YES IT IS, SIR.

SHF

WELL, IT **WAS** A RESCUE.
VWUMMM

<WE WILL TAKE THE DOCTOR.>
<BUT, BY ALL MEANS, **PLEASE** FIGHT BACK.>

GET DOCTOR LU OUT OF HERE.
WHAT ABOUT YOU?

I'LL HOLD THEM OFF.

UH. I HOPE.

<"ONE RAID, THREE FORTUNES." THAT'S A RALLYING CRY.>

<NEVER SEEN OUR MEN FIGHT SO HARD.>

<THE HELL IS THAT?!>
DAKKA DAKKA
VWOM
BKOW

<STOP!>
PHOOM

HMPHF

BRATTA TATTA TAT
<WELL, THIS IS UNEXPECTED.>

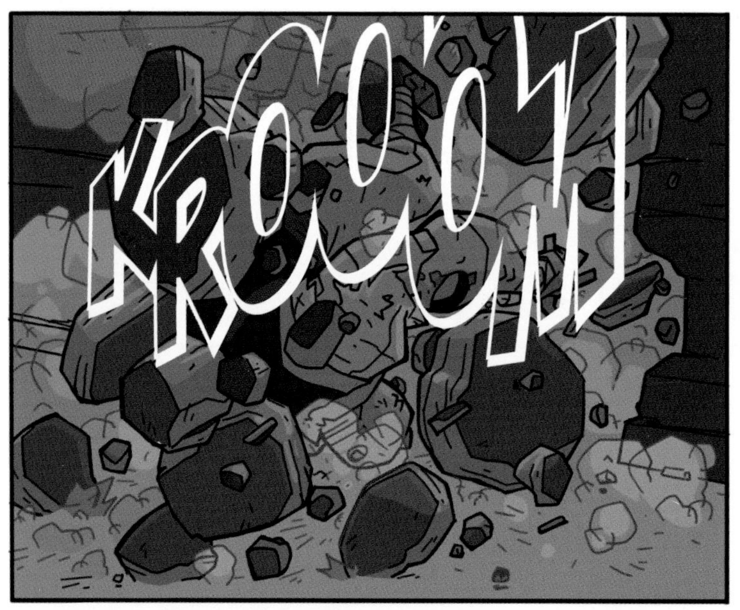
KROOOOM

<I WISH YOU SPOKE OUR LANGUAGE.>
<I WOULD TELL YOU IT DOESN'T EVEN **HURT** WHEN YOU HIT US.>

DUNNO **WHAT** YOU'RE SAYING, BUT I'M **SURE** IT'S CLEVER.

OKAY. THE OD MAKES YOU HIT LIKE **HOWITZERS.**
KTOOM
VVOM
**AND** MAKES IT IMPOSSIBLE TO HIT **BACK.**
BUT MAYBE...
...I CAN **TRICK** YOU.

KRCHOOM
AIIEEE!

<WE'RE **OUTGUNNED!**>
<DON'T WORRY. WE'RE **SURROUNDED** TOO.>
<YOU'RE A **REAL** HELP.>

<THERE, UP THE STAIRS!>
<I SEE 'EM!>
CHAKKA DAKKA CHATTA

**AUGH!**
BKOW
BLAM BLAM

BRAKKA DAK

HMMM.
CHAKKA CHAKKA

<WHERE ARE OUR DAMN **TANKS?**>

MEANWHILE, DOCTOR LU IS ALMOST RESCUED...
WHAT IF ONE OF THEM GETS LOOSE?
SHOOT 'IM.
I NEVER SHOT A GUN BEFORE.
YEAH, BUT THEY DON'T KNOW THAT.

BRUMMM

THERE WE GO. HOP IN, DOC.

WE HAVE TO GO BACK!
DON'T WORRY, NOW THAT YOU'RE RESCUED, WE CAN HEAD BACK AND RESCUE ROBO TOO.

NO, NO--THE LABORATORY!
WE MAY AS WELL SURRENDER NOW IF WE DON'T DESTROY IT.

DOC, TRUST ME. YOU WANT SOMETHING DESTROYED, YOU WANT ROBO.
SKREEE

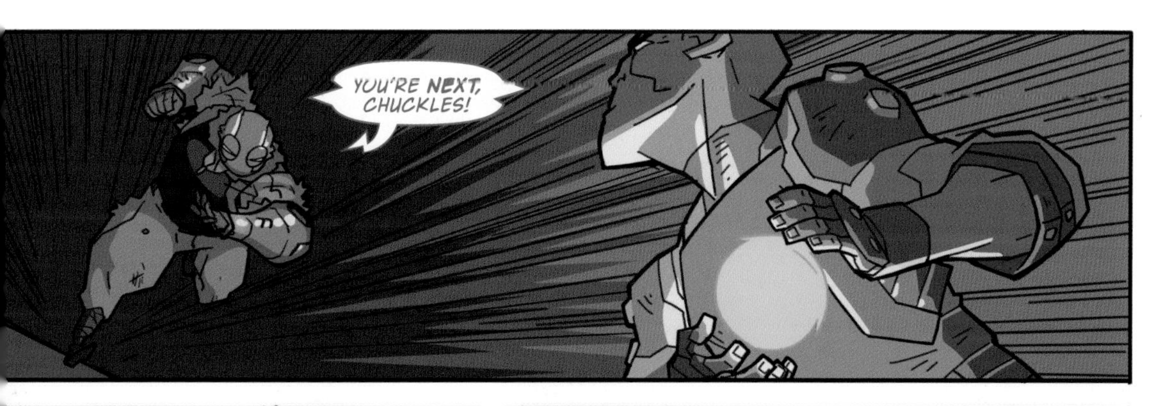
YOU'RE **NEXT**, CHUCKLES!

WOMP

VAM

SHOULDN'T THIS BE ENOUGH PRESSURE TO SNAP YOUR **SPINE** LIKE A TWIG?
THIS IS WHY I **HATE** SCI-FI WIZARDS.

VRMMM

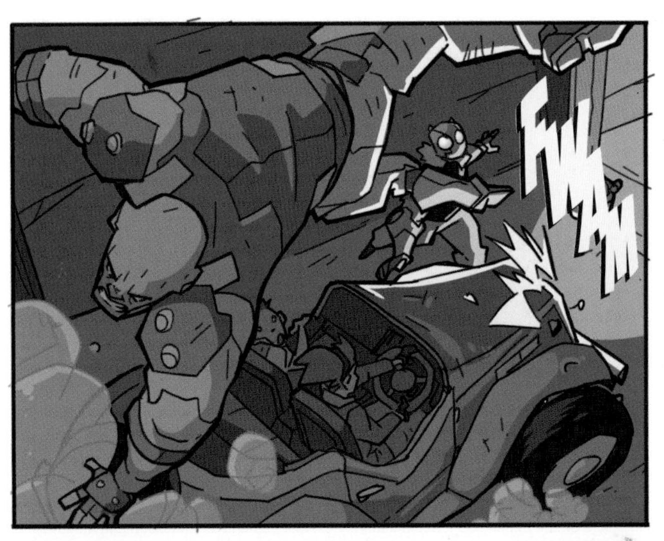
FWAM

FWUMP

AND THAT DOCTOR LU, IS HOW YOU DO A RESCUE.

HE SHRUGGED IT OFF LIKE IT WAS NOTHING WHEN I HIT HIM.

WHERE YOU HEADED, STRANGER? GOT ROOM IN THE BACK FOR ONE MORE.

THINK THIS THING CAN GET US BACK TO THE RENDEZVOUS AT GHOST CITY?

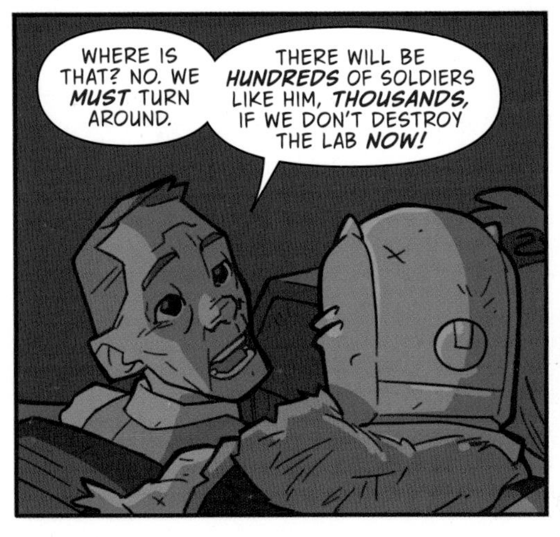
WHERE IS THAT? NO. WE MUST TURN AROUND.
THERE WILL BE HUNDREDS OF SOLDIERS LIKE HIM, THOUSANDS, IF WE DON'T DESTROY THE LAB NOW!

WE CAN WORRY ABOUT THAT AFTER WE GET YOU TO SAFETY, DOC.

<ONE OF THEM WEIRDOS IS BLOCKIN' THE WAY OUT!>
<NOT FOR LONG!>
CHATTA CHATTA
VrmmMMMM

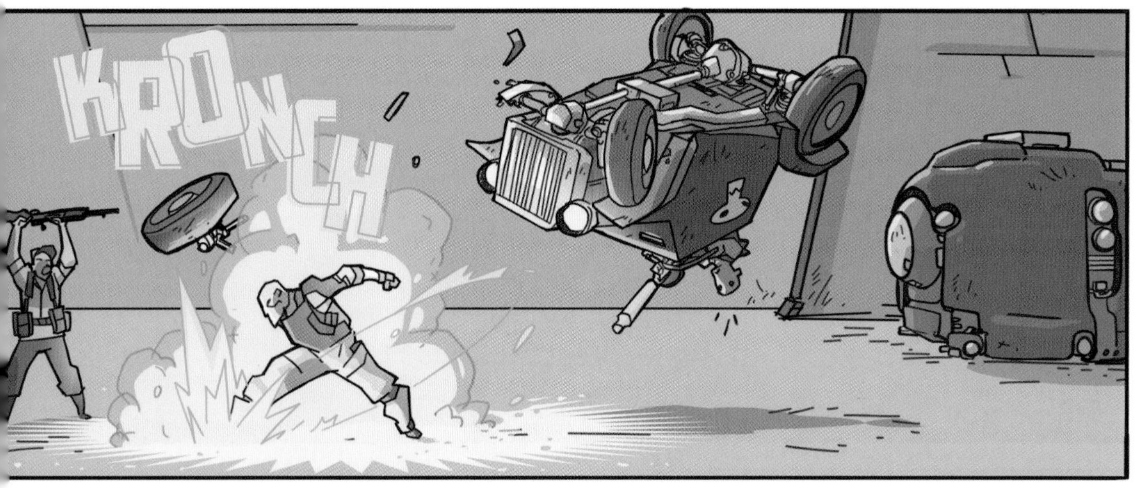
KRONCH

<WE'RE LOSING TOO MANY TRUCKS. ALSO MY HAT.>
<RETREAT!>

HEY, LOOK WHAT I FOUND. THE OUTDOORS.
VrmmM

AND JUST IN TIME, TOO.
<RETREAT! SPREAD THE WORD!>
CHAKKA CHAKKA

<DO NOT GIVE PURSUIT! SECURE THE FORTRESS!>
<PUT OUT THOSE FIRES!>
<GATHER THE WOUNDED!>

<I WANT ENGINEERS WORKING ON THIS NOW.>
<THE REACTOR COULD OVERLOAD WITHOUT IT.>

<LIEUTENANT! THE PRISONERS! THEY-->

"--THEY GOT AWAY."

<FIND THEM.>

# LET THE ZERO-POINT ENERGY FLY

3

ART BY SCOTT WEGENER
COLORS BY ANTHONY CLARK

BEIJING UNIVERSITY
JULY, 1937
<WHERE IS IT?>
<WHERE IS IT!>
<WHAT IS IT?>

<EQUATIONS, OF COURSE>
<DOCTOR LU, YOU'RE A PHYSICIST. THAT DOESN'T NARROW IT DOWN.>

<FOUND IT!>

<IS THAT EVERY-THING?>
SHF

<THERE'S A FEW NOTES LEFT, BUT THEY'RE USELESS WITHOUT A ROBUST UNDER-STANDING OF HYPERGEOMETIC RELATIVITY.>
<WHICH THEY WOULD ONLY HAVE WITH MY BRAIN OR THESE PAPERS.>

<GREAT. NOW ALL WE HAVE TO DO IS GET YOU AND THOSE PAPERS OUT OF THIS WARZONE.>

<CHEN ZHEN. SURELY YOU DON'T BELIEVE THE JAPANESE WILL ATTACK THE UNIVERSITY.>

<WHO WOULD WAGE WAR OVER A BIT OF MATH?>
<UNLESS THEY HAVE A CURIOUS TRADITION OF SIGHTSEEING FROM TANKS, THEN THEY ALREADY HAVE.>

<THEY'LL ATTACK ANYTHING TO GET YOUR ZERO-POINT ENERGY THEORY.>

<READY TO RUN, DOC?>
<WON'T THAT LOOK SUSPICIOUS?>
<VERY. SO WE'LL HAVE TO GO FAST.>

D'AH!
FWSSHH

<THAT HIM?>
<CLOSE ENOUGH.>

<DOCTOR LU!>

<RUN!>

<HALT!>

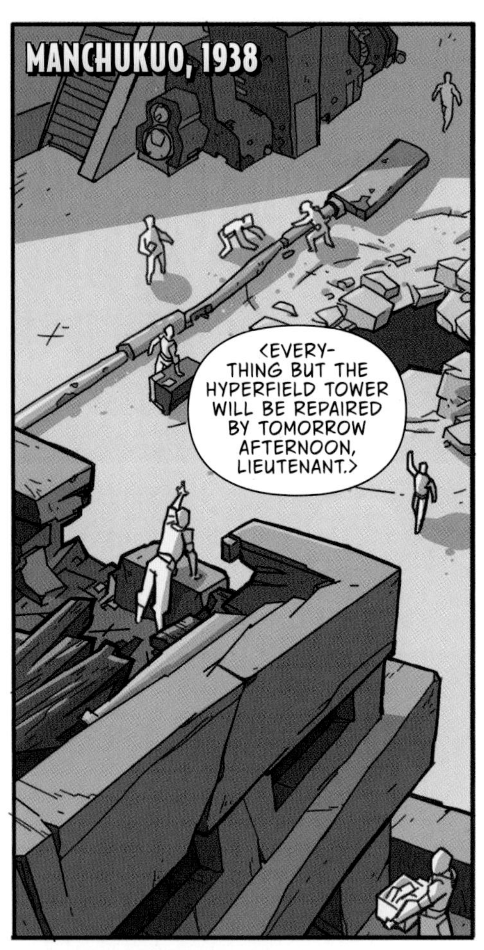
MANCHUKUO, 1938
<EVERY-THING BUT THE HYPERFIELD TOWER WILL BE REPAIRED BY TOMORROW AFTERNOON, LIEUTENANT.>

<THEY MIGHT HAVE CAUSED SOME SERIOUS DAMAGE HAD IT BEEN A COORDINATED MILITARY EFFORT.>
<THE TOWER IS CRITICAL.>
<WE CAN'T MAINTAIN ADEQUATE ZERO-POINT ENERGY LEVELS WITHOUT IT.>

<IT WILL TAKE WEEKS.>
<BUT IF WE DECIDE SAFETY IS NOT A CURRENT PRIORITY, IT CAN BE DONE BY NIGHTFALL.>

<LIEUTENANT! LIEUTENANT!>

<HMM. GHOST CITY? YOU'RE CERTAIN?>

<YES, SIR. THERE ARE GHOST BANDITS EVERYWHERE.>
<DO NOT ENGAGE. REPORT ANY NEW ACTIVITY.>

<THE GHOST BANDITS MUST BE IN LEAGUE WITH THE RESISTANCE. THEIR ATTACK WAS COORDINATED TO RECLAIM DOCTOR LU.>

<TO HELL WITH SAFETY. GET OUR ZERO-POINT REACTOR WORKING BY ANY MEANS NECESSARY. WE WILL NOT FAIL THE EMPEROR.>

GHOST CITY
SO, WE'RE SURE THESE "GHOST BANDITS" ARE ON OUR SIDE?
THEY HATE THE JAPANESE OCCUPATION ENOUGH TO COOPERATE WITH THE CHINESE RESISTANCE.

BUT CHEN SAYS HAVING THEIR COOPERATION ISN'T THE SAME AS HAVING THEIR LOYALTY.
RIGHT.
ENEMY OF MY ENEMY.

KNOCK

MATSUDA UNLOCKED INCALCULABLE POWER.
THERE'S A LOT OF THAT GOING AROUND THESE DAYS.

WE MUST GO BACK AND PUT AN END TO IT.
WE WILL, DOC. WE HAD TO GET YOU OUT OF THERE FIRST.

YOU WILL NEED MY HELP TO MAKE SURE IT'S DONE PROPERLY. NO ONE KNOWS MORE ABOUT HYPERFIELD QUANTUM MECHANICS.

AND THAT'S WHY WE'RE GETTING YOU OUT OF THERE. WE CAN'T RISK YOU FALLING INTO ENEMY HANDS AGAIN.
DON'T WORRY, DOCTOR LU. THIS ISN'T OUR FIRST TIME DEALING WITH ODIC ENERGY.

WHAT IS THIS ODIC?

AN ENERGY FIELD UNDERLYING ALL LIFE. MAYBE REALITY ITSELF. EDISON THOUGHT IT'D MAKE HIM IMMORTAL.
IMMORTALITY.
HADN'T CONSIDERED THAT.

<WE LOST GOOD MEN ON THAT RAID! ALSO MY HAT.>
<AND FOR WHAT!>

<FOR THIS?>
<WE CAN'T EVEN SELL HIM!>
<I MEAN. WE CAN, THOUGH.>

<HAHA!>
<SHUT UP.>

WHAT'S HAPPENING?
THE GHOST BANDITS ARE EXTORTING US.

<IT'S *YOUR* FIGHT, BUT *WE'RE* THE ONE'S SUFFERING FOR IT!>
<THE RESISTANCE SHOULD *PAY* FOR OUR LOSSES!>
<*PLUS* THE FINDER'S FEE. *AND* EXFILTRATION. *AND* ROOM AND BOARD. *AND* AROUND THE CLOCK PROTECTION.>
<ARE YA DONE?>

<THE OCCUPATION'S WORSE FOR *YOU* THAN ANYBODY BECAUSE *NOW* WHAT PASSES FOR *LAW* OUT HERE HAS *TANKS.*>
<SO, IF IT'S *ANYTHING,* IT'S THE *RESISTANCE* THAT'S HELPING *YOU.*>

<WELL. YOU *STILL* OWE US FOR THROWING OUR GUYS AGAINST THOSE SPOOKY WEIRD POWERS.>

<WHAT SPOOKY WEIRD POWERS?>
TF

ZHEN!
SORRY IT TOOK SO LONG TO CATCH UP.

I KNEW YOU'D MAKE IT.
LIAR.

GLAD YOU COULD JOIN US, CHEN.

SOUNDS LIKE I'M JUST IN TIME TOO. WHAT'S THIS BUSINESS ABOUT SPOOKY POWERS?
MATSUDA PRODUCED A **WORKING** HYPERFIELD ENGINE.

<SO SOON? **HOW?!**>
<MATSUDA IS JAPAN'S TOP MAN IN QUANTUM MECHANICS. HE HAS MY PAPERS ON THE ZERO-POINT, IT WAS INEVITABLE.>
<HIS SOLDIERS ARE IMBUED WITH **LIMITLESS** ENERGY.>

<**WE** KNOW HOW TO FIGHT 'EM.>
<BUT IT AIN'T FREE.>
<YOU'RE LUCKY. WE'RE RUNNING A DISCOUNT ON SPECIAL INTELLIGENCE THIS WEEK.>

ARE THEY BEING HELPFUL? THEY **SEEM** LIKE THEY'RE BEING HELPFUL.

<THAT'S YOUR BIG STRATEGY?>
HANG ON. WHAT'S HAPPENING HERE? WHY ARE WE UPSET?

THEY SAID TO HIT THEM FROM BEHIND.
<IT WORKS.>
<PROBABLY IT WORKS.>
<PAY.>

THEY'RE WASTING OUR TIME.
NO, WAIT. THEY'RE RIGHT.

THOSE GUYS TOOK EVERY PUNCH I HAD LIKE IT WAS NOTHING, BUT HELEN TOOK ONE OUT WITH A SINGLE HIT.
YEAH, WITH A CAR, ROBO.

MY PUNCHES ARE LIKE GETTING HIT BY A CAR. THE DIFFERENCE IS, HE DIDN'T SEE YOU COMING AT HIM.
I THINK THEIR ZERO-POINT ENERGY IS USELESS WITHOUT INTENT TO GUIDE IT.

<SO. SURPRISE ATTACKS, EH?>
<WORKS EVERY TIME.>
<MOST TIMES, PROBABLY.>

<BOSS! THE DAMN **RUSSIANS** ARE HERE!>
THE RUSSIANS!

WHAT'RE **THEY** DOING HERE?
<THEY SHOW UP ALL THE TIME.>

<THEY ONLY WANT TO DRINK AND GAMBLE AND BE A **NUISANCE** BECAUSE THEY'RE **RUSSIAN.**>
<WE HAVE TO HIDE YOU.>
<WE'LL ADD IT TO YOUR BILL.>

DO WE **TRUST** THESE GUYS?
THEY CAN'T KEEP BILLING US IF WE'RE **DEAD.**
WHY IS **NO ONE** GOOD AT ASSURANCES IN THIS GROUP?

HOW ABOUT THIS FOR ASSURANCE? I'LL STAY BEHIND SO WE'VE GOT SOMEONE KEEPING AN EYE ON THINGS.
JUST BE CAREFUL.

HEY. I'M **ALWAYS** CAREFUL.
LIAR.

THAT EVENING...
NO, NO. IT WASN'T UNTIL THE 1927 SOLVAY CONFERENCE.
YOU WERE THERE, DOCTOR LU?

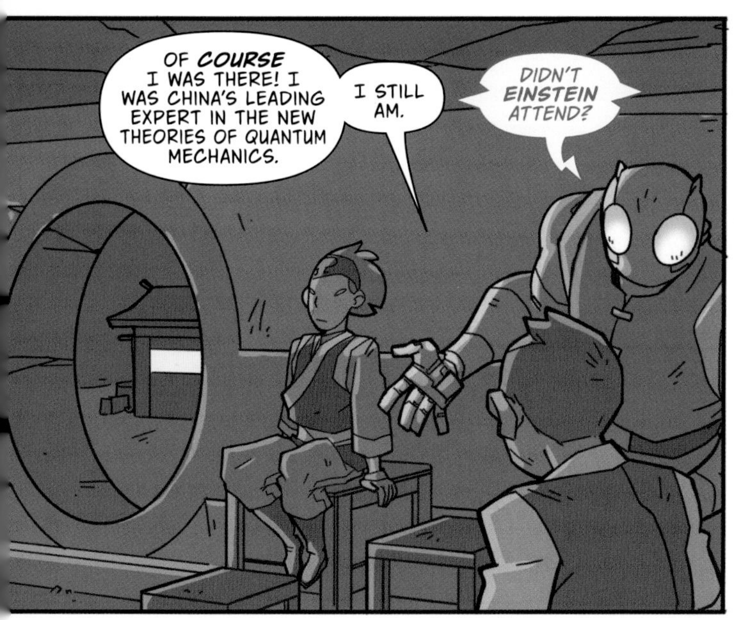
OF COURSE I WAS THERE! I WAS CHINA'S LEADING EXPERT IN THE NEW THEORIES OF QUANTUM MECHANICS.
I STILL AM.
DIDN'T EINSTEIN ATTEND?

OH, YES. AND BOHR, AND PLANCK, AND CURIE. QUITE A GATHERING OF GENIUS. THERE WAS A PICTURE IN MY OFFICE.
I SUPPOSE THE JAPANESE HAVE IT NOW.

AND THAT'S WHERE YOU THOUGHT OF ZERO-POINT ENERGY?
NOT QUITE. I WAS WORKING ON THE OBSERVATION PROBLEM.
THERE WAS A GREAT DEAL OF DEBATE ABOUT IT AT THE CONFERENCE, YOU UNDERSTAND.

OUR EXPERIMENTS SHOWED QUANTUM EFFECTS WERE ALTERED SIMPLY BY OBSERVING THEM.
AND THAT IS PRECISELY THE PROBLEM, ISN'T IT.
HOW COULD MATTER OR ENERGY "KNOW" WHEN IT IS OBSERVED?

MY THINKING WENT LIKE THIS.
CONSCIOUSNESS IS A PROPERTY OF THE **BRAIN.** THE BRAIN IS **MATTER** AND **ENERGY.**
EINSTEIN'S MODEL DESCRIBES MATTER AND ENERGY AS SPACETIME. AS **GEOMETRY.**
THEREFORE, **CONSCIOUSNESS** CAN BE SEEN AS A PHENOMENON OF A SUFFICIENTLY COMPLEX SPACETIME MATRIX. A **HYPERFIELD.**
AS SUCH, MENTAL STATES, THE SELF, PERCEPTION, EVEN **KNOWLEDGE,** OUGHT TO BE SUBJECT TO PHYSICAL LAWS.

I SPENT TEN YEARS MAPPING A HYPERGEOMETRIC MODEL OF THE MIND TO EXPLAIN HOW PHYSICAL LAWS MIGHT BE SUBJECT TO CONSCIOUSNESS.
IN THEORY, A PROPERLY AUGMENTED **HYPERFIELD** COULD ALLOW A MIND TO CONSCIOUSLY **INFLUENCE** REALITY RATHER THAN MERELY **PERCEIVE** IT.

DUNNO IF WE CAN STILL CALL THAT **THEORETICAL,** DOC.

*SO, MATSUDA'S USING HYPERFIELDS TO CREATE LIMITLESS ENERGY JUST BY **THINKING** ABOUT IT?*
NO. HYPERFIELDS DO NOT CREATE. THEY **BORROW** FROM THE LOWEST ENERGY STATE OF THE UNIVERSE. WHAT WE CALL THE **ZERO-POINT.**
CLASSICAL PHYSICS **ASSUMES** THIS TO BE **ZERO** ENERGY. THERE OUGHT TO BE NOTHING TO BORROW. YES?
BUT QUANTUM MECHANICS SUGGESTS THE ZERO-POINT IS **ACTUALLY** A VAST **OCEAN** OF ENERGY PROPPING UP THE UNIVERSE ITSELF.

GUESS MATSUDA PROVED THAT ONE RIGHT.
YES. IT'S QUITE A VICTORY FOR QUANTUM MECHANICS. BUT IT ALSO TURNED MY LIFE'S WORK INTO A **WEAPON.**

Y'KNOW, I'M MORE **ENGINEER** THAN **PHYSICIST,** BUT IT OCCURS TO ME THAT **MATH** IS **MATH.** RIGHT?
IF YOU MADE A SUPERPOWER **EQUATION,** THERE'S GOT TO BE ANOTHER ONE TO CANCEL IT OUT.

I SUPPOSE THERE IS.
*THAT COULD TAKE **YEARS** TO FIGURE OUT. WE'VE GOT TO STOP MATSUDA **NOW.***

OUR RUSSIANS ARE BEGINNING TO WIND DOWN. MOSTLY BY PASSING OUT.
SO, HERE'S THE PLAN.

MATSUDA HAS TWO PRIORITIES. TO REPAIR THE DAMAGE WE DID AND TO FIND US. THE SOONER WE STRIKE, THE LESS PREPARED HE'LL BE FOR IT.
WE'LL HEAD OUT AS SOON AS THE RUSSIANS ARE OUT OF COMMISSION. SHOULD BE ANOTHER HOUR OR SO.

YOU TWO WILL TAKE DOCTOR LU BACK TO A RESISTANCE SAFE HOUSE WHILE I HEAD BACK WITH THE GHOST BANDITS TO DEMOLISH MATSUDA'S LAB.

I DON'T LIKE IT.
ME EITHER.
WELL, THAT MAKES THREE OF US. BUT WE DON'T HAVE A CHOICE.

MATSUDA'S BOUND TO HAVE SOME OF THOSE HYPERFIELD GOONS IN RESERVE.
ROBO'S THE ONLY ONE WHO CAN GO TOE-TO-TOE WITH THEM.

IF THERE ARE ANY. WHICH SEEMS UNLIKELY AFTER OUR RAID. THE REAL PROBLEM IS WE CAN JUST BARELY TRUST THE GHOST BANDITS.

THEY'RE ONLY WORKING WITH US BECAUSE THEY WANT THE JAPANESE OUT. BUT THAT DOESN'T MEAN THEY REALLY WANT US TO BE HERE EITHER.
IF THEY CAN GET RID OF BOTH, SO MUCH THE BETTER. AND, BELIEVE ME, THEY'RE THINKING ABOUT HOW RIGHT NOW.
ROBO'S GOT NO CHANCE OF STAYING ON TOP OF THAT UNLESS HE LEARNED TO SPEAK MANCHURIAN WHILE I WAS OUT
I DIDN'T. IF ANYONE'S WONDERING.

SO, WE'RE BACK WHERE WE STARTED. YOU WITH THE GHOST BANDITS, ME AND ROBO WITH LU.
LIKE I SAID, I'M NOT HAPPY ABOUT IT EITHER.

JUST PROMISE ME YOU'LL BE SAFE.
ONLY IF YOU DO THE SAME.
OKAY.
OKAY.

LIARS.

<IT IS NEARLY SUNRISE>
<IT IS, SIR.>
<YOU ASSURED ME OUR ZERO-POINT REACTOR WOULD BE ONLINE BY NOW.>

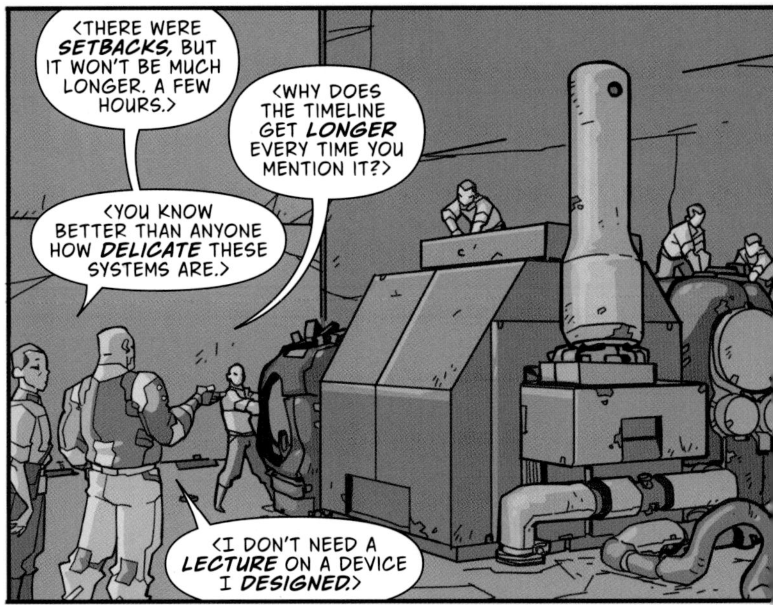
<THERE WERE SETBACKS, BUT IT WON'T BE MUCH LONGER. A FEW HOURS.>
<WHY DOES THE TIMELINE GET LONGER EVERY TIME YOU MENTION IT?>
<YOU KNOW BETTER THAN ANYONE HOW DELICATE THESE SYSTEMS ARE.>
<I DON'T NEED A LECTURE ON A DEVICE I DESIGNED.>

<YOU KNOW WE CAN ONLY WORK SO FAST WITHOUT RISKING DAMAGE TO THEM.>
<AND OUR TECHNICIANS. AND, UH, LOCAL SPACETIME.>
<A FEW HOURS, YOU SAY?>
<MORNING AT THE LATEST.>
<REPORT FROM OUR SCOUTS, SIR.>

<MATSUDA. GO AHEAD.>

<RUSSIAN SOLDIERS ARE **STILL** HERE.>
<MAKING A **HELL** OF A RACKET TOO.>

<ARE THEY SEARCHING FOR DOCTOR LU?>
<WE HAVE REASON TO BELIEVE IT IS A **RECREATIONAL** VISIT, SIR.>
<OF COURSE IT IS.>

<RAISE THE ELITES. DIRECT THEM TO A FIRING POSITION UPON GHOST CITY.>
<SIR!>

THE ELITES
<WE CAN BE THERE IN TWO HOURS.>

<WE NEED THE ZERO-POINT ENERGY REACTOR ONLINE.>
<YOU HAVE **ONE** HOUR.>

SPANRANG

ONE HOUR LATER...

FINALLY.

WE **MUST** GO BACK AND **DESTROY** MATSUDA'S LABORATORY.
NO, **WE** MUST GET YOU OUT OF DANGER.

CHEN AND THE GHOST BANDITS CAN TAKE CARE OF THE LAB FOR US.
EASILY. MATSUDA'S GOT NO ADVANTAGE OVER US WITHOUT HIS REACTOR. AND HIS MEN ARE SPREAD THIN SCOURING THE BADLANDS FOR US.

EVEN SO. DON'T PLAY HERO.
BACK AT YOU.

<BEGIN THE ATTACK.>

BOOM

BA-THOOOM
BA-THOOOM
<CEASE FIRE. MOVE IN.>

HEY, ZHEN. I THINK THEY FOUND US.
GET DOCTOR LU **OUT** OF HERE! WE CAN HANDLE THIS AS LONG AS--

--EXACTLY **THAT** DOESN'T HAPPEN.
I'M **NOT** LEAVING YOU IN THE MIDDLE OF THIS.
BUT DOCTOR LU!

YOU'RE **BOTH** TAKING HIM. **GO!**
**ROBO!**

C'MON, Y'MOOKS.
FWAM

I'M GIVING THAT ROBOT A **STERN** TALKING-TO IF WE ALL LIVE THROUGH THIS.
BIG "IF."

STRAP IN, DOC.
BOOM
BOOM

OKAY, YEAH. YOU'RE SUPER STRONG.
fwmp

BUT SO AM I.

HANG ON!
VROOOOM

KRAKOOOM!
AUGH!

FWAM

THE SHELLING STOPPED. THEY MUST NOT WANT TO BLOW UP THEIR OWN PEOPLE.

THAT MEANS ROBO'S SAFE!

I WOULDN'T GO *THAT* FAR.

JUST GOTTA TAKE THEM BY SURPRISE!
WUNK

BUT

SHOULDA THOUGHT

HOW

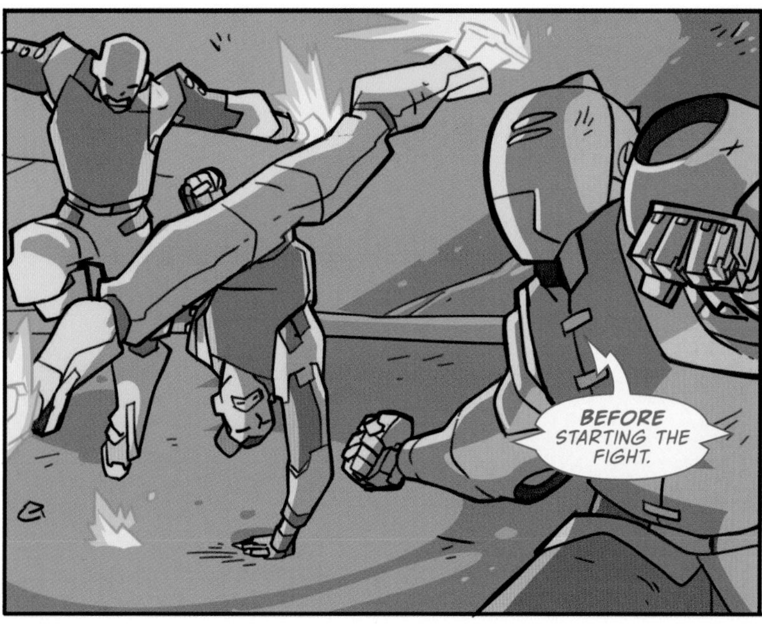
BEFORE STARTING THE FIGHT.

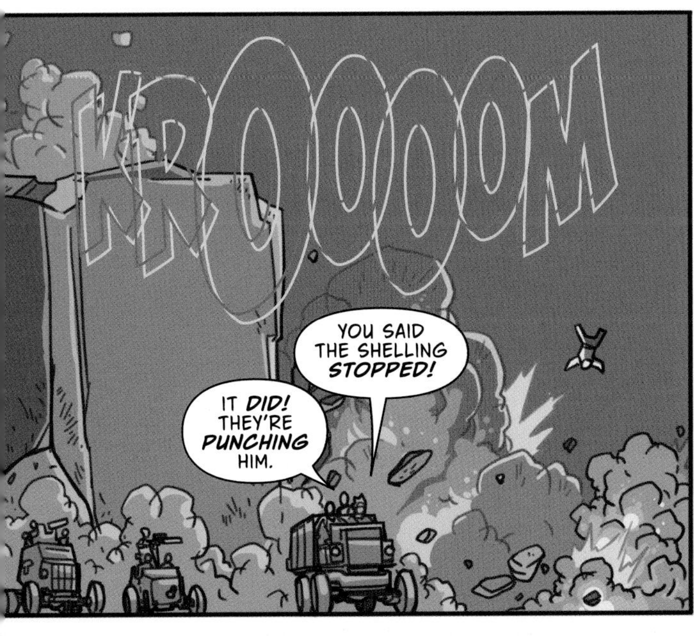
VROOOOOM
YOU SAID THE SHELLING STOPPED!
IT DID! THEY'RE PUNCHING HIM.

WHYYYY.

<YOU WILL SEE HIM JUST WEST OF THE FORT. FIRE.>

GOT 'EM.
WHERE I WANT 'EM.

WRRR
WRRR
WRRR

KA-BOOOM
BA-BOOM

THEY.
THEY GOT ROBO.

I'M SORRY, HELEN. I DON'T...
HELEN?

HELEN!

BRAKES!

AAAAHHHH!!

# MILES OF HYPERDIMENSIONAL FLAME

4

ART BY SCOTT WEGENER
COLORS BY ANTHONY CLARK

TOKYO IMPERIAL UNIVERSITY, 1928
<WHAT DID THEY *TEACH* YOU IN BERLIN, MR. MATSUDA?>

<QUANTUM MECHANICS, SIR.>

<WE ARE *QUITE* FAMILIAR WITH QUANTUM MECHANICAL THEORY, MR. MATSUDA.>
<FRANKLY, WE'D HAVE *WELCOMED* ITS APPEARANCE IN YOUR PAPER.>

<I AM THE FIRST TO ADMIT MY WORK IS *UNCONVENTIONAL.* EVEN BY THE *WILDLY* ECCENTRIC STANDARDS OF QUANTUM THEORY.>
<BUT I BELIEVE WE CAN LEARN MORE ABOUT THE COSMOS BY *INVESTIGATING* OUTLANDISH IDEAS THAN BY *REGURGITATING* ORTHODOXY.>

<A *MAVERICK* WE COULD TOLERATE. *NOT* A MADMAN.>
<DO NOT MAKE THIS BOARD REGRET ITS DECISION TODAY, *DOCTOR* MATSUDA.>

RIKEN INSTITUTE, 1932

<YOU WANTED TO SPEAK WITH ME, DOCTOR NISHINA?>
<DID YOU KNOW THE AMERICANS HAVE BUILT A PARTICLE ACCELERATOR? THE "CYCLOTRON.">

<AMAZING.>
<IT IS.>
<DON'T YOU THINK WE SHOULD HAVE OUR OWN?>
<ABSOLUTELY. MY THEORIES WILL NEVER BE PROVEN WITHOUT ONE.>

<THERE ARE SOME WHO THINK NOTHING WILL PROVE YOUR THEORIES, MATSUDA.>
<NOT ME, OF COURSE. I ONLY CONSIDER YOUR THEORIES RIDICULOUS.>
<THAT'S WHY I WANT YOU TO HELP DESIGN OUR CYCLOTRON. IT'S A RIDICULOUS PROJECT. IT WILL REQUIRE RIDICULOUS IDEAS.>

<IT'LL BE EXPENSIVE.>
<VASTLY.>
<WHO'S PAYING FOR IT?>

RIKEN INSTITUTE, 1935

<WHO ARE-->
<DOCTOR MATSUDA?>
<I'LL ASK THE QUESTIONS.>

<NO. YOU WON'T.>
<WE FEEL YOUR WORK IS WASTED ON NISHINA'S CYCLOTRON.>

<WHAT DO YOU KNOW OF MY WORK?>
<ANTI-GRAVITY. ELECTRIC ARTILLERY. TELE-TRANSPORTATION.>


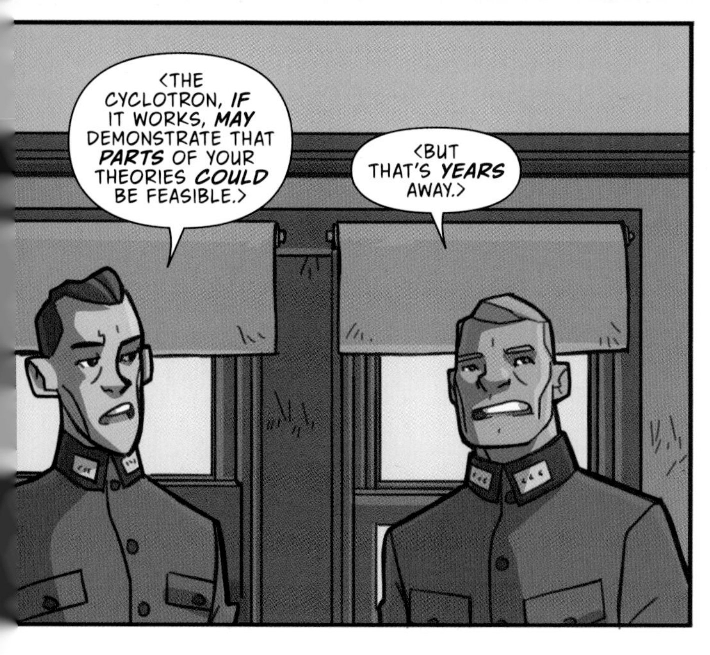

<THE CYCLOTRON, IF IT WORKS, MAY DEMONSTRATE THAT PARTS OF YOUR THEORIES COULD BE FEASIBLE.>
<BUT THAT'S YEARS AWAY.>

<WHEREAS THE IMPERIAL NAVY'S CHOKAITEN PROJECT NEEDS YOU TODAY.>

MANCHUKUO, 1938
I DON'T SEE WHY THEY DON'T JUST *KILL* US.
OH, DON'T WORRY. THEY *WILL.*
BUT *FIRST* MATSUDA HAS TO LET US KNOW THERE'S NO *HURRY.*

IT'S PURE *EGO* IS WHAT IT IS.
SO *WE* KNOW *HE KNOWS* HE'S WON.

<QUIET!>

<DOES THAT APPLY TO *ME* AS WELL?>

VWUMM

<WE NEED THAT ONE.>

<WHAT HAS HE DONE...?>

MISS MCALLISTER, DOCTOR LU. WELCOME BACK.
YOU BROUGHT A ***FRIEND?*** I BELIEVE WE CAN FIND SOME ROOM FOR HIM.
OH, QUIT ***GLOATING.***

YOUR RESISTANCE IS ***DESTROYED,*** AND WITH DOCTOR LU ***CAPTURED,*** ONLY ***WE*** WILL POSSESS THE SECRET OF ZERO-POINT ENERGY WEAPONS.
I'M NOT ***GLOATING.*** I ***WON.***

WHAT IS THIS LIGHT? WHAT HAVE YOU ***DONE?***
HYPERFIELD LEAKAGE CRYSTALLIZING LOCAL SPACETIME.

AND YOU WILL HELP US FIX IT BEFORE IT BECOMES ***HAZARDOUS.***

GHOST CITY
THE HELL HIT ME.

KUNK
KUNK

<WE LOST OUR HOME!>
<ONE OF 'EM, ANYWAY.>
<WE LOST GOOD MEN.>
<SOME OF 'EM, ANYWAY.>
<DO YOU THINK HE SPEAKS ANYTHING LIKE A NORMAL LANGUAGE?>
<MANCHU? JAPANESE? MONGOLIAN? KOREAN? MANDARIN?>

UM. I DON'T KNOW WHAT YOU'RE SAYING?

<WHAT'S HE SAYING?>
<DAMN FOREIGNERS. ANYONE STILL **ALIVE** SPEAK ENGLISH?>

**YEAH, YEAH. HOWDY OKAY.**
<WHAT WAS THAT?>
<TRADITIONAL AMERICAN GREETING.>

<WHEN'D YOU LEARN ENGLISH?>
<I HAVE HIDDEN DEPTHS.>
<AND YOU NEVER THOUGHT TO **TELL** US?!>
<WOULDN'T BE **HIDDEN** THEN, WOULD IT?>

THE WAY I FIGURE IT, MATSUDA'S OUR **REAL** ENEMY.
AND **NEITHER** OF US GET WHAT WE WANT IF WE FIGHT EACH OTHER **INSTEAD**.

<HE'S **BROKE**, BUT HE HAS A PLAN TO GET THE **JAPANESE** TO PAY US.>
<QUESTION IS, DO WE GET MORE **HELPING** HIM OR **SELLING** HIM TO THE JAPANESE?>

<YOU WILL FIX IT.>
<I WILL DO NO SUCH THING.>
<YES YOU **WILL**, DOCTOR LU.>
<OUR HYPERFIELDS ARE LEAKING. LOCAL SPACETIME IS **DESTABILIZING.** YOU'VE SEEN IT YOURSELF.>
<AND YOU KNOW IT WON'T STOP HERE. THE FABRIC OF REALITY **ITSELF** WILL BE UNRAVELLED BEFORE IT'S OVER.>

<THEN TURN **OFF** YOUR ZERO-POINT REACTOR.>
<YOU WOULD LIKE THAT. BUT NO.>

<THIS IS YOUR CHOICE.>
<DO **NOTHING** AND YOUR TECHNOLOGY WILL **DESTROY** THE WORLD.>
<OR **FIX** YOUR DEVICE LET ME BRING **ORDER** TO THE WORLD.>

FIRST SOVIET MONGOLIAN ARMY GROUP
<COMMANDER ZHUKOV!>

<SIR! SCOUTS ARE REPORTING FROM GHOST CITY.>
<LET'S HEAR IT.>
<THERE'S NOTHING LEFT BUT SMOKE.>

<AND OUR *ORIGINAL* RECON UNIT?>

<NO SIGN OF THEM, SIR.>
<BUT OUR SCOUTS FOUND JAPANESE TANK TRACKS BEARING TOWARD THE "HIDDEN FORTRESS" RESEARCH STATION.>

<JAPANESE TANKS AT OUR BORDER? A CLEAR VIOLATION OF THE CEASEFIRE!>
<AND ***ALL*** THE JUSTIFICATION REQUIRED TO FINALLY MOBILIZE AGAINST THEIR LITTLE FORTRESS.>
<THEY ARE BUILDING EXPERIMENTAL WEAPONS THERE. I'M SURE OF IT.>
<WEAPONS THAT MUST ***NEVER*** BE DEPLOYED AGAINST RUSSIA. I WILL SEE TO THAT.>

OKAY. THIS IS IT.
MY FRIENDS' **LIVES** AND YOUR BIG **PAYDAY** HANG IN THE BALANCE. ARE WE CLEAR ON THE PLAN?

<JUST SMILE AND NOD OR HE'LL KEEP TALKING.>

IT WON'T BE EASY, MEN. BUT SURPRISE IS ***EVERYTHING.***

GUYS?

IS THIS ***DYNAMITE?!***

I KNOW IT'S NOT REAL DYNAMITE.
CAUSE THAT'D BE CRAZY.
AND IT'D KILL YOU TOO. AND WE'RE ON THE SAME TEAM.

THREE FORTUNES, ONE RAID
PART TWO

<STAND DOWN! DROP YOUR WEAPONS!>

<DO WE LOOK ARMED?>

<WE GOT THE ROBOT. HE'S YOURS FOR A PRICE.>

ONE HOUR LATER...
<GENTLEMEN!>

<I HOPE YOU CAN FORGIVE MY GUARDS.>
<IT WOULD EMBARRASS ME TO NO END WERE THEIR VIGILANCE MISTAKEN AS AN INSULT.>

<YOU'LL PAY IN BLOOD!>
CHAK
KCHK
CH-CHK

BY THE WAY, IT WAS **ALL** A TRICK.
CHATTA CHATTA

SHRRP

<***GUNS?*** THE FABRIC OF REALITY IS ***ENSLAVED*** TO MY ***WILL*** AND YOU BROUGHT ***GUNS?***>

FSSSS

THAT WAS REAL DYNAMITE?

KRABOOOOM
THAT WAS REAL DYNAMITE?!

WAS THAT AN EXPLOSION?
IT WAS. ROBO'S ALIVE.

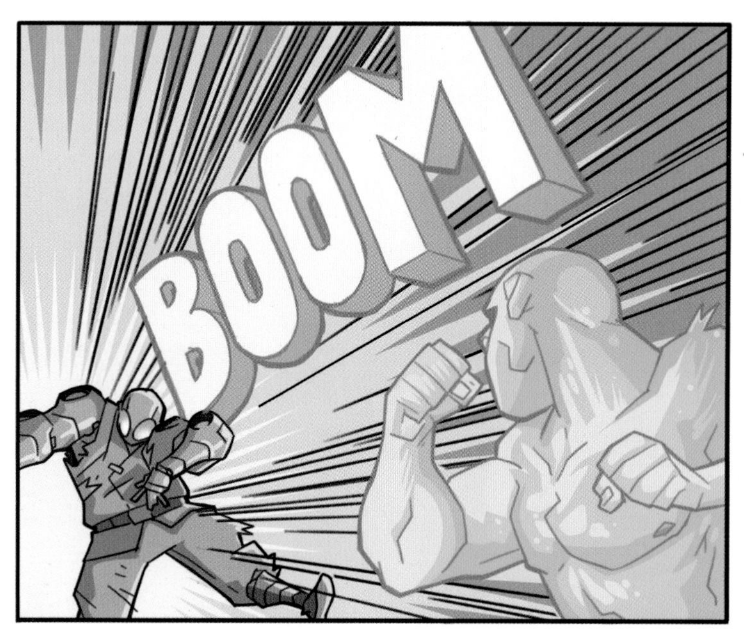
BOOM

THIS IS A **CONVOLUTED** MEANS OF COMMITTING **SUICIDE,** ROBO.

YEAH? I'M SURE THE REALITY-WARPING ENERGY YOU **SHOVED** INTO YOUR **ORGANS** IS WORKING OUT **FINE.**

KZAK
IT'S WORKING **WONDERS.**

AND IT'S ONLY GETTING **BETTER.**
I CAN SEE THROUGH **TIME,** ROBO.

**BRAIN TUMORS** CAN MAKE YOU THINK ALL **KINDS** OF CRAZY THINGS, MATSUDA.

<GUARD! YOU'VE GOT TO HELP US!>

<OH NO. IS SOMEONE SICK? I BETTER UNLOCK THE DOOR!>
<GIVE ME A BREAK.>

<OKAY, BUT MATSUDA NEEDS THIS GUY ALIVE, AND I'M NOT SURE HOW LONG THAT'LL LAST SINCE THE CEILING ATTACKED HIM.>
<YOU REALLY WANT TO BE THE GUY MATSUDA BLAMES WHEN HE DIES?>

<DON'T NEED THIS AGGRAVATION.>

WUMP
DOOF
THUD
<YOU WERE RIGHT TO SUSPECT US.>

MEANWHILE, RUSSIANS
<YOUR ORDERS, COMMANDER ZHUKOV?>

<OPEN FIRE AND DO NOT STOP UNTIL NOTHING REMAINS.>

THERE'S NO SHAME IN THIS DEFEAT, ROBO. YOU NEVER HAD A CHANCE.

FWABOOOM

KABOOOM

RUSSIANS!

BOOOM
KABOOOM
WE HAVE TO FIND DOCTOR LU.
THEN WE HAVE TO FIND THEIR REACTOR.

THOOOM
AND WE HAVE TO DO IT BEFORE THIS PLACE FALLS IN ON US.

WE'D COVER MORE GROUND IF WE SPLIT UP.
AND ***THEN*** WE'D NEVER FIND EACH OTHER.
B-BOOOM

HANG ON.
THEY'VE STOPPED?

<SOMETHING'S WRONG. THE EXPLOSIONS STOPPED.>
THOOM

SHFFFF

KRABOOOM

THE SHACKLES OF THE MATERIAL UNIVERSE ARE UNDONE.
TIME AND SPACE OBEY MY EVERY COMMAND, ROBO.
SWELL.

HOW CAN YOU HOPE TO STOP ME WITH YOUR LITTLE LINEAR MIND?

CAN YOU TELL ME WHAT IT IS ABOUT ULTIMATE POWER THAT MAKES EVERYONE TALK LIKE THAT?

<YOU SURE ABOUT THIS?>
<NO. BUT ANYTHING THAT CAN LIVE THROUGH THIS MUCH DYNAMITE WAS GONNA KILL US ANYWAY.>

<REMEMBER. I GET TRIPLE PAY IF I LIVE.>
<IT WAS DOUBLE!>
<YOU WANNA DO THIS?>
<TRIPLE IT IS.>

<SHOULDA PUSHED FOR QUADRUPLE.>

LOOK AT YOU.

CRAWLING THROUGH TIME.
VWORP

<NOW!>
RRRNK

WWOR-TOOM

# THE HIDDEN TEMPLE

5

ART BY SCOTT WEGENER
COLORS BY ANTHONY CLARK

IMPERIAL JAPANESE HIDDEN FORTRESS
MANCHUKUO, 1939
WELL. I DON'T KNOW WHAT *ANY* OF THIS IS...

...BUT IT LOOKS LIKE *EVERYTHING* WE HAVE TO *BREAK*.
WHAT ABOUT DOCTOR LU? *AND* THE GUARDS?

*I'LL* KEEP THE GUARDS BUSY. *YOU* FIND DOCTOR LU.

FWUMP

BLAM
BLAM BLAM

BLAM BLAM

CHATTA CHATT
KICK
BLAM BLAM BLAM
BLAM

CHAKKA CHAK

DUNF
BLAM

SHE MUSTN'T DAMAGE THE EQUIPMENT!

YOU WANTED TO DESTROY THE LAB, DIDN'T YOU?
YES! BUT IT'LL REND THE EARTH IN HALF IF IT ISN'T DONE PROPERLY!

WELL. *THEY'RE* DEAD.

FOOLISH GIRL!
I'M SORRY, WOULD YOU RATHER GO BACK TO THE *DUNGEON?*
HE'S JUST UPSET BECAUSE THE EARTH *MIGHT* BE DOOMED.

NOT IF *I* CAN HELP IT. BUT IT WILL REQUIRE *TIME.*

NOT SURE THAT'S AN *OPTION,* DOC. REINFORCEMENTS WILL BE HERE ANY MINUTE.
DOC. WE *JUST* FOUND YOU. WE *CAN'T* SPLIT UP.
*NOT* IF YOU LEAD THEM *AWAY* WITH A *LOT* OF GUNFIRE.

YOU'RE RIGHT. BUT DO YOU HAVE A *BETTER* IDEA?
I DON'T.

DOC, YOU KNOW YOUR WAY AROUND. MEET US IN THE GARAGE AS *SOON* AS YOU'RE FINISHED HERE.
YES, YES. *GO.*

<ARE WE ALIVE?>
<TOO SOON TO TELL.>

<YOU NEARLY KILLED ME!>
<IT WASN'T A TRIPLE PAY HAZARD JOB BECAUSE IT WAS EXTRA SAFE.>
<HEY. WE'RE ARGUING. WE'RE DEFINITELY ALIVE.>

DID WE GET HIM?

HUAAAUGH.

I'LL TAKE THAT AS A NO.

<NOW WE'RE DEAD.>

SHOULDA BROUGHT MY LIGHTNING GUN.

FWOMP

APPLESAUCE.

WHAT HAVE YOU DONE?

VVVRA
AIIIEEE!

VWORMP
UH.

VWUMPF

ZWORPF
WAIT--
--WHAT?

WHAT HAVE YOU DONE!
HEY. REMEMBER WHEN YOU DID THIS TO YOURSELF?

THRAKOOOM

MATSUDA, WHAT HAVE YOU DONE?
BARELY ENOUGH ENERGY LEFT IN THE SYSTEM TO SUSTAIN THE ZERO-POINT SIPHON. WHERE IS IT ALL GOING?

COMPLETE HYPERGEOMETRIC COLLAPSE IS INEVITABLE.
EARTH ITSELF WILL BE OBLITERATED.

I DON'T KNOW WHAT THIS DOES.
IF I COULD ADJUST THE ZERO-POINT REACTOR TO TUNNEL ITS MELTDOWN OUTSIDE OUR UNIVERSE...

...THAT MIGHT BE ENOUGH TO MINIMIZE DAMAGE TO LOCAL MINKOWSKI SPACE.

<THIS ISN'T AN ESCAPE, IT'S SUICIDE!>
<IT'S ONLY SUICIDE IF IT KILLS US!>

<I WANT A NEW GANG LEADER.>

TIME IS THE *SHADOW* OF CONSCIOUSNESS!

OH, MY GOD.

SHUT UP!

ZWORPT
D'AH!

THE PRESENT IS AN ILLUSION OF THE PAST *REFRACTING* INTO THE FUTURE.
LINEARITY IS THE *FICTION* OF THE *LENS.*

YOU SURE WE'RE GOING THE RIGHT WAY?
THEY BROUGHT US THROUGH THE GARAGE THE FIRST TIME I WAS CAPTURED.
AND YOU DEFINITELY REMEMBER WHERE IT IS?
MOSTLY DEFINITELY, YEAH.

I SHOULDN'T COMPLAIN, BUT WHERE'S THE OPPOSITION?
YEAH. THIS PLACE WAS TEEMING WITH TROOPS. WHAT GIVES?

EITHER THERE'S BEEN A COMPLETE BREAKDOWN IN COMMAND.
OR THERE'S A BIG AMBUSH AND WE'RE ABOUT TO RUN RIGHT INTO IT.

YOU'RE LOSING YOUR MIND!

THE MIND IS A TANGLE OF WORMS STRETCHED ACROSS ETERNITY!

STOP BEING SO WEIRD!
VUMP

ZWORP

KTONG

WELL. WE FOUND THE GARAGE.
SO DID THEY.

ONE RAID, HALF A FORTUNE

KLIK-
KLA-
KLIK

VMMMM
OH, I HOPE IT'S SUPPOSED TO BE DOING THAT.

<WE DON'T WANT TROUBLE.>
<NOR DO WE.>
<GOOD.>
<GREAT.>

<RAIDING THEIR ARSENAL JUST IN CASE WE LIVE THROUGH THIS THING. SMART.>
<BUT HOW DO YOU PLAN TO GET OUT OF HERE WITH IT?>

vrrumble

<LET'S GO. I DON'T WANNA GET KILLED JUST 'CAUSE IT'S THE END OF THE WORLD.>

<WE NEED A RIDE.>
<IT'LL COST YOU.>
<WHAT A SURPRISE.>

<WELL? GET IN.>
<WE HAVE TO WAIT FOR DOCTOR LU.>
<NO DEAL.>

<WE'LL PAY *EXTRA.*>
<DEAD MEN DON'T PAY ANYTHING.>
<*ALL* THIS WAS FOR *NOTHING* IF WE LEAVE WITHOUT HIM.>

<*WE* ARE LEAVING. NOW.>
<YOU WANT TO WAIT? STEAL YOUR OWN TRUCK.>

<REAL FUNNY.>

<HE *SAID* WE'RE *WAITING* FOR DOCTOR LU.>

DEAD WORMS. NOTHING BUT DEAD WORMS EATING STARLIGHT.

THAT'S GREAT.
YOU KNOW YOU'RE GOING CRAZY AND BECOMING INCORPOREAL?

ZRAAAAKOW

SHHKROOOOM

WHY CAN'T THE ENERGY BE INCORPOREAL TOO?

ROBO!
<GOOD THING WE WAITED SO WE CAN GET KILLED NOW.>

YOU NEED TO GET OUT OF HERE. NOW.
NOT WITHOUT DOCTOR LU!

GREAT.
I CAN BUY YOU BETWEEN ONE AND ZERO MINUTES.

THE UNIVERSE IS NOTHING BUT DUST SINGING ITS OWN DIRGE.

CAN'T YOU SLAP ME AROUND WITHOUT TALKING CRAZY?

<WHAT'S HE DOING?!>
<GIVING US ONE SHOT.>

YOU WOULD SPEAK TO ME OF INSANITY?
VWORPT

LOOK AT YOU. A PATCHWORK OF LONG DEAD STARS CRAWLING THROUGH TIME LIKE A WORM.
FWAM

HOPING THE LITTLE DREAMS OF YOUR LITTLE CONSCIOUSNESS WILL STALL OBLIVION. THAT IS INSANITY.
OKAY. BUT YOU'RE THE ONE ABOUT TO BE BLOWN UP BY WORMS.

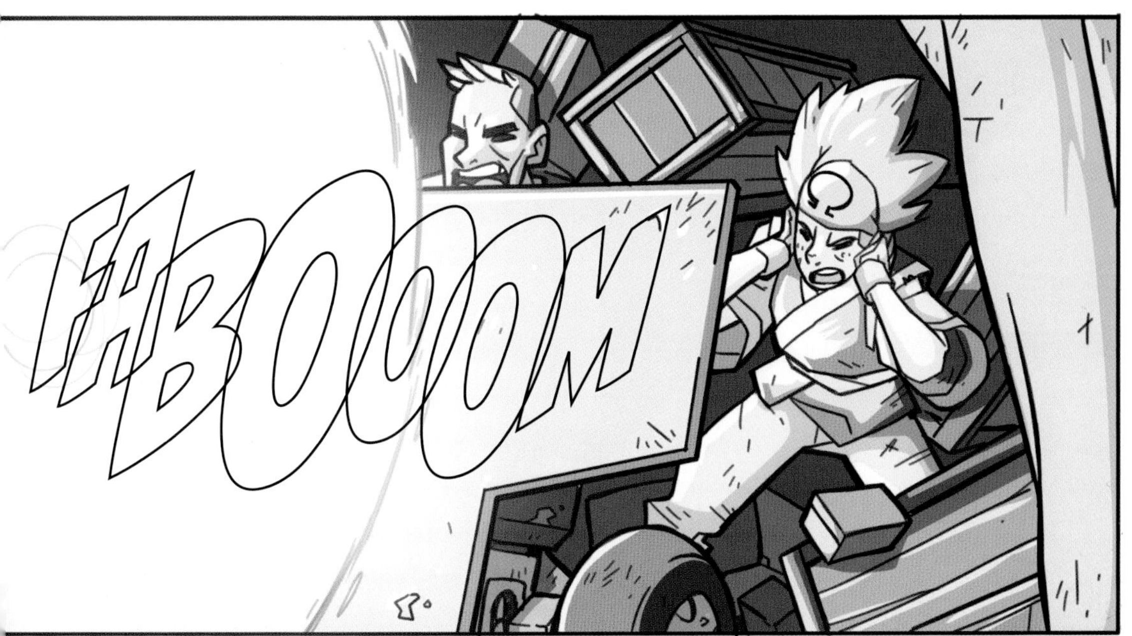
FABOOOM

SURELY THAT WAS NOT YOUR FINAL PLAN.

KCHUNK

UH. KINDA WAS. YEAH.

PLAN B?
HOPE FOR A QUICK DEATH.

IT IS DONE.

SHMMMMMMMMMMMMM
MY THEORY IS NOT A WEAPON.

SHMMMMMMMMMMMMMMMMMM

WWWORPF

HUAAAAARGH!

GOSH.
WHO COULD'VE GUESSED TOYING WITH THE FABRIC OF THE UNIVERSE COULD END IN RUIN?

ROBO!
vrooOOm

kchonk-a-chonk

<MAYBE YOU SHOULD DRIVE **FORWARD.**>
<YEAH, YEAH.>

SHHHHFF

S'OKAY. JUST MY **PRIDE,** MY **FACE,** AND MY **BODY** THAT GOT HURT.

ZZKROOOM

DOCTOR LU! NEVER SHOULD'VE LEFT HIM BEHIND.
HE TOLD US TO.
THIS IS WHAT HE WANTED.

IT WAS THE ONLY WAY HE COULD GUARANTEE THIS WOULDN'T HAPPEN TO HIS THEORIES AGAIN.

SO, UH. THIS ENERGY SYPHON THING. IT'LL STOP, RIGHT?
EITHER YES OR WE'RE ABOUT TO FIND OUT WHAT A SCHWARZSCHILD RADIUS LOOKS LIKE.
THAT'S ONE OF THOSE HORRIBLE ASTROPHYSICAL LIMITS WHERE REALITY BREAKS DOWN, ISN'T IT.
HEY, CAN THIS THING GO ANY FASTER?
KRAKBOOOOM

WORMS.
STARLIGHT.

DUST.

!
NOW WHAT?
I'M THINKING BEIJING. GET BACK WITH THE RESISTANCE AND SEE WHERE THAT TAKES US.

IT'S US, IS IT?

ISN'T IT?
IT IS.

OH, COME ON!
YOU DON'T EXPECT ME TO WALK ALL THE WAY BACK TO KUNMING, DO YOU?!

<WHAT'S HE SAYING?>
<HE'S GONNA HIRE US TO SMUGGLE HIM ACROSS A WARZONE.>
<HAZARD PAY!>

RUINS OF THE HIDDEN FORTRESS
<GATHER ALL THAT REMAINS. BODIES, WRECKAGE, EVERYTHING.>
<WE MUST LEARN ALL WE CAN ABOUT THIS JAPANESE SUPERWEAPON.>

MPERIAL GENERAL HEADQUARTERS
<VERY WELL.>

<THERE IS NO TRACE OF DOCTOR MATSUDA OR HIS RESEARCH FACILITY.>
<NO MATTER.>

<WE HAVE MATSUDA'S NOTES. THIS IS NOTHING BUT A TEMPORARY SETBACK FOR THE CHOKAITEN PROJECT.>

<REMEMBER.>
<THERE IS NO FORCE ON EARTH SO CLOSE AS WE ARE TO DEVELOPING ZERO-POINT ENERGY WEAPONS.>

KUNMING, THREE WEEKS LATER
ROBO.

I READ YOUR REPORT.
DAMN SHAME ABOUT LU.
YES, SIR.

STILL. MISSION ACCOMPLISHED.
READY FOR THE *NEXT* ONE?

YES, SIR.
THE END

# VARIANT COVER GALLERY

ART BY GIANNIS MILONOGIANNIS

MACLEAN
2016
ART BY ANDREW MACLEAN

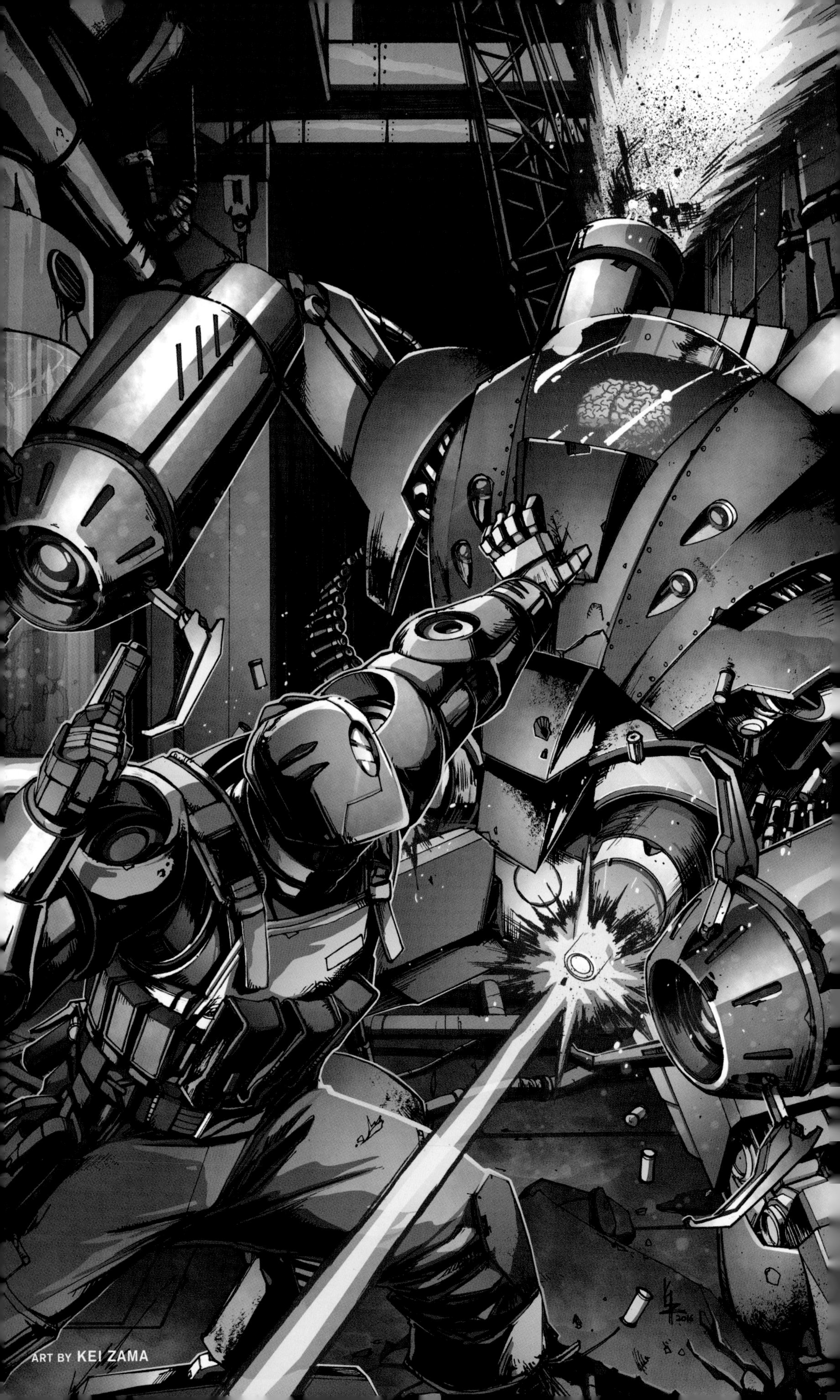

ART BY KEI ZAMA

ART BY HOLLIE MENGERT

ART BY DAVE CROSLAND

# FROM TESLADYNE LABS

Like all great movies, the only way to improve upon *The Good the Bad the Weird* or *Let the Bullets Fly* is to throw a robot into them.

So that was the plan for this volume.

It would mean, however, dipping back into the World War 2 era. It's a goldmine of pulp adventure yarns, of course, but these days you gotta go pretty deep into the mine to find a vein.

We always knew we had to do one WW2 story. How could we have a super robot running around history without throwing him at it, right? So we dove into it with our second volume, *The Dogs of War*. We chose to focus on smaller parts of the conflict practically unknown in pop consciousness to minimize potential rehashiness, so you got stories in occupied Croatia, the invasion of Sicily, and the Channel Islands instead of NORMANDY NORMANDY NORMANDY.

It's been eight years (good lord) and we still haven't done another World War 2 story. We will, one day, but *Atomic Robo and the Temple of Od* ain't it, barely, since it takes place months before the invasion of Poland marks the official start of the war. You may call that a technicality, but TOO LATE YOU ALREADY BOUGHT IT AHAHAHA!

Still, we wanted to highlight parts of the (pre-) war that go mostly overlooked. Much of our story takes place in occupied Manchuria, officially renamed Manchukuo by the Imperial Japanese forces who did the occupying. They were there, and in Korea and bits of Mongolia, as part of their overall invasion of a China severely weakened by a decade of Civil War caused by a long story of corruption and suffering. And then there's Russia's reactions to all this stuff, not the least of which was to develop a post-WW1 tank doctrine before anyone else. There's a lot of history in this region, is what I'm saying, even when we confine our survey to a few years of the 20th century. And we're never taught any of it.

Without a robust investigation into history it becomes easy to think the shape of the modern world is natural. Even inevitable. It's a notion that puts hard limits on what you are able to imagine about what the world could be or what it perhaps ought to be. We hope our robot adventure comics inspire a spark of interest in discovering a few of your own hidden corners of history.

Brian Clevinger
RVA, 2017

Another year has come and gone, my beard is a bit grayer, and you've just read another volume of Atomic Robo. If America doesn't degenerate into an '80s B-movie dystopia under the new proto-fascist administration, I look forward to bringing you more stories about a robot who loves punching Nazis in the face.

Scott Wegener
RVA, 2017